HOT SEAL, HAWAIIAN NIGHTS

BROTHERHOOD PROTECTORS

ELLE JAMES

TWISTED PAGE INC

HOT SEAL, HAWAIIAN NIGHTS

SEALs in Paradise
and
Brotherhood Protectors

New York Times & *USA Today*
Bestselling Author

ELLE JAMES

EBOOK ISBN: 978-1-62695-247-8

PRINT ISBN: 978-1-62695-248-5

Dedicated to the beauty of Hawaii and the people who call it home. Aloha!

Elle James

AUTHOR'S NOTE

Enjoy other military books by Elle James

Brotherhood Protectors Series

Montana SEAL (#1)
Bride Protector SEAL (#2)
Montana D-Force (#3)
Cowboy D-Force (#4)
Montana Ranger (#5)
Montana Dog Soldier (#6)
Montana SEAL Daddy (#7)
Montana Ranger's Wedding Vow (#8)
Montana SEAL Undercover Daddy (#9)
Cape Cod SEAL Rescue (#10)
Montana SEAL Friendly Fire (#11)
Montana SEAL's Mail-Order Bride (#12)
Montana Rescue
Hot SEAL, Salty Dog
Hot SEAL, Hawaiian Nights

Visit ellejames.com for more titles and release dates and join Elle James and Myla Jackson's Newsletter at Newsletter

CHAPTER 1

"HAWK, you old son of a bitch. I can't believe you're jumping ship on us." Nitro clapped Hawk on the back and shook him hard. "The team won't be the same without you."

Jace Hawkins, or Hawk to his friends, stood in the lounge of a small municipal airport southeast of San Diego. He glanced around at the members of his team who'd come to see him off, nostalgia kicking in. *Damn*. And he hadn't even left yet. Still, the thought wasn't lost on him. This would be the last time he'd be with SEAL Team 3, his friends and brothers in arms.

"Seriously," Dutch said. "Who's going to cover my six when we're out on the town? I can't depend on Zach and T-Bone." He elbowed T-Bone in the gut. "They'll ditch me for any girl shortsighted enough to go after them."

"You're a grown-ass man, Dutch, you know how to call for a ride back to your apartment." Jace glanced down at his watch. In exactly five minutes he'd be on a chartered jet to Bozeman, Montana to meet up with his old friend and new boss Hank Patterson, owner of the Brotherhood Protectors security agency.

God, it would be good to be back home. San Diego had great weather year-round, but Hawk liked his home in Eagle Rock with its wide-open spaces and snow-covered mountains.

Being a Navy SEAL had been his dream for as long as he could remember. After thirteen years of constant deployment, never being able to put down roots or find someone who could put up with his absences, he couldn't wait to settle into a real house on a ranch. He looked forward to working with cattle and horses and riding for long stretches without another soul in sight.

He could already smell the pine trees. How nice would it be not to fight California traffic and inhale smog every day? Or to actually see the stars at night instead of all the light pollution caused by streetlights, parking lot floodlights and security lights hung on every front porch? Montana was as close to paradise as a man could get. And if ranching wasn't enough to keep him busy, his new occupation should be a lot less dangerous than being a Navy SEAL, fighting the good fight all over the world.

Home sweet home.

He sighed.

"You know, after you've given civilian life a shot, you're gonna get bored." Dutch crossed his arms over his chest. "I bet the Navy would take you back."

Hawk shook his head. "Have you ever been to Montana?"

Justus raised his right hand. "I have. I stopped at one of the insanely few truck stops on my way through from Minneapolis to Seattle. Montana was a long, straight stretch of absolutely nothing." He snorted. "Until I hit the mountains. They don't call it the Big Sky state for nothing. On the plains, that's all there is, flat land and blue skies. Not a single tree for hundreds of miles. The only saving grace is the mountains in the far western part of the state. That's where it got interesting."

Hawk grinned. Justus's description sounded like pure heaven. "And that's where I'm headed. The Crazy Mountains and the little town of Eagle Rock." Hawk inhaled deeply. "Can't wait to get there. Just a few more hours and I'm there."

Zach shook his head. "I don't like that you and Compass are breaking up the team."

"All good things come to an end," Compass said. "Savannah has been on my mind for so long, it's time to go."

"Nothing will be the same," Justus grumbled. "We'll have to train some new guy. It took me years to train you two."

Hawk laughed at the youngest man on the team. "The fuck, you did. *We* trained *you*. It's your turn to initiate some poor, dumb bastard into the team."

Justus frowned. "Is that all I was to you when I came on board? Some poor, dumb bastard?"

"Damn straight, you were." Hawk punched the guy in the shoulder. "All our training—"

"—hazing," Justus corrected.

"—came in handy," Hawk continued. "You saved my ass on more than one occasion."

"And mine," Zach Browne added.

"Mine, too," Dutch contributed. "But it goes both ways."

Justus rubbed his shoulder. "Yeah, well at least it'll be nice to have someone else to pick on." He nodded toward the plane taxiing toward them. "That your ride?"

Butterflies swarmed in Hawk's gut as he stared out at the shiny white plane stopping in front of the building. The hatch dropped down, and a man dressed in a pilot's uniform stepped out.

Zach whistled. "Patterson must be making a mint with his security agency to afford a plane like that."

Hawk frowned. He'd expected a much smaller, single prop plane to pick him up. "Might not be my plane."

Hawk's teammates stood beside him as the pilot entered the building, carrying a leather portfolio. His gaze swept the faces of the men in front of him. "One of you Jace Hawkins?"

Hawk's pulse leapt. "That's me." He stepped forward.

"Hank Patterson sent this for you." He handed the leather folder to Hawk, bent to collect Hawk's suitcases and started for the sliding door out to the tarmac. "Follow me, please," he said over his shoulder.

Hawk stared down at the black folder and up at the pilot passing through the door. "Well, guys, I guess this is it."

"Damned impressive, if you ask me," Zach said. "When you see Patterson, put in a good word for the rest of us. Might not be a bad gig when we're done with the Navy." He wrapped his arms around Hawk in a tight hug then stepped back. "See ya around."

Justus was next. "Don't fall off any cliffs in those mountains of yours."

"Ride 'em hard and put 'em up wet," Nitro said, hugged him and then gave him a fist bump.

T-Bone held out a hand. Hawk took it and was pulled into a bone-crunching hug. *"Laissez les bon temps rouler,"* T-Bone said in Cajun French. "Let the good times roll. You will be missed."

Once he'd said his goodbyes, Hawk slung his backpack over his shoulder, waved and followed the pilot out the door and up the steps to the waiting jet being fueled by a tanker truck.

Hawk was amazed at the luxury of the interior. "Are you sure you're here for me?" he asked the pilot who'd handed him the folder.

The man retracted the steps into the plane and sealed the door. "Patterson said everything you need to know is in that folder. And he wants you to call him before we take off. That gives you about five minutes until we're done refueling and get clearance. Sit anywhere you like. The flight will be about five and a half hours." He stepped into the cockpit next to another pilot.

"It takes that long to fly to Bozeman?"

The pilot frowned. "Bozeman?"

Hawk felt like a character in the Twilight Zone. "Yeah, Bozeman. As in Montana."

The man was shaking his head before Hawk finished talking. "I don't know anything about Bozeman,

Montana. We're flying from here to Kona, Hawaii. As I said, everything you need to know should be in that brief. If you have any questions, save them for Hank Patterson."

Hawk glanced at the now sealed hatch. Was it too late to get off the plane? Kona, Hawaii? What the hell was going on? He had his heart set on going home. And home sure as hell wasn't on the Big Island of Hawaii.

In a state of shock, Hawk sat in one of the white leather seats and pulled out his cell phone. Patterson's number was at the top of his favorites list. He punched the number and waited for the man to answer, opening the briefing materials at the same time.

"Hawk, you should be boarding the jet about now. Am I right?" Hank Patterson's voice sounded in his ear.

"What the hell's going on?"

"Didn't the pilot give you the brief?" Patterson asked.

"I'm opening it now. But give me the bottom-line up front. Why am I headed to Hawaii? I thought I'd be working in Montana."

Patterson laughed. "You will. But I had an emergency assignment come up, and everyone else is assigned. Sorry I couldn't be there to welcome you to the Brotherhood Protectors in person, but I'm on babysitting duty with my little girl, while my wife is on the set of her latest movie shoot."

"But...Hawaii?" Hawk said, hoping to bring Patterson back to the point.

"Right. I actually got a call from one of your buddies on SEAL Team 3. His girlfriend's family friend from back in Hawaii is in a tight spot. Someone attempted to kidnap the daughter two days ago. They failed, but her father is afraid they'll try again."

"And why am I the right man for the job?" Hawk shook his head. "I know nothing about Hawaii, other than it has palm trees and hula dancers."

"You know more than you think." Patterson chuckled. "The Big Island has a massive cattle ranch smackdab in the middle of it. The family owns the ranch, all one hundred and thirty thousand acres."

Hawk blew out a stream of air. "You're kidding me."

"I kid you not." Patterson continued, "We think whoever tried to kidnap the daughter wants to use her for ransom. The family is loaded. Her father chartered the plane. He's pretty desperate."

"I'd say." Hawk stared around at his luxurious transportation. "So, all I have to do is play bodyguard to the man's daughter?"

"Yes…and no."

"You're not making sense." Hawk stared down at the first sheet in front of him with a description of Parkman Ranch. "Either I'm a bodyguard, or I'm not."

"You'll be the daughter's bodyguard, but you can't let her know you're a bodyguard. Her father says she's a bit of a free spirit and has slipped free of every bodyguard he's hired. He wants you to come on board as a ranch hand, working with the horses. She's not to know you're her bodyguard."

Hawk frowned. "She sounds like a spoiled brat. What doesn't he just spank her and make her behave?"

Patterson laughed out loud. "You'll have to ask him. I take it he's not into disciplining his daughter." A baby cooed in the background on Patterson's end of the communication. "Having a baby daughter of my own, I can understand his hesitation to discipline. Isn't that right, Emma?"

A tiny giggle sounded in Hawk's ear. Was Patterson the same badass SEAL he'd known back in BUD/S training?

"Has the plane taken off yet?" Patterson asked.

"Not yet. They're fueling up."

"You have the opportunity now to change your mind, if you don't think you can do the job. But you're the only man I have available at this time, and Parkman's desperate to protect his daughter..." Patterson paused, giving Hawk time to reconsider.

Hawk blew out a breath. "No, I've got this. Hell, it's a free trip to Hawaii. Who'd be stupid enough to turn that down?" *Someone who'd prefer to be in Montana.* Given that this would be Hawk's first assignment as a Brotherhood Protector, he couldn't turn down work. He had to prove he was ready, able and, most of all, willing to do whatever it took.

"I know how much you wanted to get back to Montana," Patterson said. "I wanted to get back home when I left the Navy. I could juggle my guys and switch one of them off a current assignment if you'd like."

"No. I'm on the plane, it wouldn't make sense to disrupt anyone else on your team," Hawk squared his shoulders. "You can count on me."

"Thanks, Hawk. You've got my number. If you need anything, call, and enjoy Hawaii as a civilian." Patterson ended the call before Hawk had a chance to change his mind.

For better or worse, he'd just accepted his first assignment. In Hawaii. Not Montana.

Hawk sat back against the plush leather, buckled his seatbelt and prepared himself for the long flight over the water to the Big Island.

He tamped down his disappointment and looked down at the information Patterson had provided. In it was a map of the Big Island and a plat map of Parkman Ranch. So, it wasn't Montana. Lots of people would love to fly in a private jet to Hawaii. Also included was the Parkman family tree, dating all the way back to the mid-1800's. The last person on the tree was John Parkman III's daughter Kalea. From the dates on the tree, Kalea's mother had passed several years earlier. Which explained why John Parkman struggled with disciplining his only daughter. If Hawk had only one living relative, he'd probably feel the same.

He sighed. Hell, he was usually pretty good with the kids of his teammates. How hard could it be to protect little Kalea Parkman from kidnappers?

CHAPTER 2

KALEA RACED ACROSS THE PASTURE, hunkering low in her saddle. She was supposed to have been back at the ranch house by five o'clock for her weekly hula lesson. Her father would be livid. She'd promised to be there after missing her lesson the previous week altogether. She'd tried telling her father that she had no interest in learning the native dance of her mother's ancestors. It was boring, and she'd been doing the dance since she was small child. Why did she have to practice? So, she was a little rusty. She could improvise as she always had for the annual Parkman Ranch celebration.

With the huge barn in sight, she leaned over *Pupule's* neck, urging the gelding to run faster.

When she arrived in the barnyard, she barely waited for the horse to slide to a halt before she leaped out of the saddle to the ground.

"Where have you been, *ali'i?*" Maleko Hakekia reached up to grab her horse's bridle. "Your father is looking for you."

"Is he mad?" Kalea asked, leading *Pupule* toward the barn.

"He's not happy," Maleko responded. "I'll take your horse. Your father's expecting you at the house."

"I always take care of my own horse," she argued. Now that she was back to the barn and knew her father was looking for her, Kalea was in no hurry to get to the house.

She knew her father loved her, but sometimes, he was too controlling, always wanting to know where she was, demanding she be at certain places according to *his* schedule. All she wanted was to help with the ranching duties, not the social responsibilities of being a Parkman of Parkman Ranch. He was so much better at that side of the business than she was. And now that he'd hired Clarise Sanders as his marketing expert, he didn't need Kalea to be there for every function. She was prettier and more poised. And she actually *liked* wearing dresses and high heels.

Just the thought of wearing heels and a dress gave Kalea the hives. She preferred her cowboy boots, jeans and a T-shirt any day.

"*Ali'i*, you need to go to your father," Maleko insisted. "He is expecting you."

Kalea sighed. "I suppose." She frowned. "And Maleko?"

"Yes, *ali'i*?"

"Don't call me princess. I don't like it. Never have. I work as hard as any man on this ranch. Calling me princess is demeaning."

Maleko nodded. "As you wish."

Kalea left *Pupule* with Maleko, not feeling at all good about having asked Maleko to stop calling her *ali'i*, the Hawaiian word for princess. He'd called her that all her life, as a term of endearment. He meant no harm, and he loved her as his own. She sighed. She shouldn't take her bad mood out on Maleko. He was as dear to her as her own father. Determined to make it up to him when she came back down to the stables that evening, she hurried up to the house and the chewing out she expected and deserved.

As she entered through the back door, she could hear her the murmur of her father's voice coming from the study. She hoped he wasn't with Lani, her hula instructor, making excuses for his daughter's tardiness.

Kalea walked as lightly as she could in her cowboy boots, trying not to make any more noise than she had to. Maybe her father was having a business meeting with someone, and she could slide by and get to the dance studio her mother had commissioned with the intention of training her daughter in the ways of her people.

As she neared the door, she heard her father and the sound of another male voice. This one was deep, resonant and a little sexy. A voice she didn't recognize. She eased around the doorframe to see who was visiting her father in his study.

A tall man with a short haircut and broad shoulders stood in front of her father. He wore jeans, fairly new cowboy boots and a white, button-down shirt. In his hand, he held a cowboy hat.

Kalea looked around the room, expecting to see a

woman dressed in the latest fancy western clothes, ready for her Hawaiian dude ranch experience on Parkman Ranch. When she didn't find the man's spouse standing nearby, her curiosity got the better of her, and she entered the study.

Her father looked up and smiled. "Speak of the devil. Hawk, I'd like you to meet my daughter, Kalea."

The man turned with a smile that immediately dropped into a frown. As quickly as the frown appeared, it disappeared behind a straight poker face. He held out his hand. "Jace Hawkins. Most folks call me Hawk."

Kalea wondered why his expression had changed so radically in the matter of seconds. "Nice to meet you Hawk," she said as she placed her hand in his.

His fingers curled around hers in a firm grip, sending a startling jolt of awareness up her arm and into her chest. The man was attractive in a rugged, outdoorsy way. Hell, she'd met lots of men who were guests or worked on the ranch. None of them had produced such a visceral reaction. She pulled her hand free and rubbed it along her dirty jeans.

Her father glanced up at the clock on the wall. "I sent Lani home with your apologies. She'll be back tomorrow at the same time. I assured her that you would be waiting…on time."

Kalea nodded. "Yes, father. Is there anything you need from me before I go shower for dinner?"

"As a matter of fact," her father said with a smile, "there is."

The way her father dragged out his words made

Kalea wary. He was up to something and, based on the way he was acting, she probably wasn't going to like it.

Her father took a deep breath and announced, "Hawk is our newest *paniolo*."

Kalea's eyebrows rose. "Is he?" She gave the tall man a skeptical glance. "What experience do you have with cattle and horses?" She let her gaze travel over him, assessing him from a different perspective than that of a prospective guest.

"I grew up on a ten-thousand-acre ranch in Montana."

"Growing up on a ranch doesn't necessarily mean you can *work* a ranch." Her gaze shot briefly to her father.

He nodded.

Her attention shifted back to the tall, good-looking man in front of her. He could prove to be a distraction. "Can you ride a horse?"

He nodded. "I learned to ride a horse when I was two."

This didn't impress Kalea. So had she. "Ever wormed a cow or horse?"

"Both."

"Tagged or branded?" she shot back.

"Both."

"Castrated a steer?" Her eyes narrowed.

"Hundreds," he said, without missing a beat.

"Have you ever roped a calf?"

"Many times. For work purposes as well as for rodeo, until I joined the military."

Her father chuckled. "I've already interviewed and hired him. No need to put him through the paces again."

Her cheeks heated. By questioning the new *paniolo*, she was insulting her father's intelligence and ability to select good help. "My apologies."

"I know my way around horses and cattle," Hawk said. "I can do the job."

Kalea inhaled and let the air out slowly. "Okay, then. I'll have Maleko show you to the bunkhouse."

Her father shook his head. "I've invited Hawk to stay at the main house in the blue room, for the time being."

Kalea's gaze turned to her father. "Why?"

"I want him to work with you."

Her gaze narrowed. "You've never wanted any of the *paniolos* to work with me. You always had Maleko show them the ropes."

Her father shrugged. "You keep telling me to give you more responsibility. I guess it's about time I did. After all, you're almost thirty."

"Like that's a magic number?" She snorted. "I have real work to do."

"I can keep up," Hawk said, "if that's what you're worried about."

She ignored Hawk and turned her full attention on her father. "Is this about that little incident that happened last week in Hilo?" She glared at Hawk. "You're not the latest bodyguard my father keeps insisting on hiring, are you?"

Hawk raised both hands. "Hey, I'm here to work with animals, not babysit the boss's daughter. I got out of the military to work with animals, not people."

She stared at him for a long moment, willing him to crack that poker face of his. Finally, she turned her ire toward her father. "Well? Is he?"

Her father spread his hands wide. "I gave up hiring bodyguards. You have a talent for evading them. Hawk is here to work the ranch. As a former Navy SEAL, who has served his country heroically, I didn't feel right sticking him out in the bunkhouse. He deserves a little better than that, don't you think?"

"A Navy SEAL?" Her brows rose. She'd heard about the SEALs when she'd been a student at the university she'd attended in San Diego. "And you want to be a *paniolo*?" She shook her head. "Seems like a step down from such an elite force."

His eyebrows lowered. "Look, lady, I've spent the last thirteen years pretty much on call twenty-four-seven. I've deployed to almost every continent in the world and been involved in enough conflicts with people killing people to last a lifetime. I'm ready to take a step back and work with animals." He gave a hint of a smile. "They don't tend to shoot at you. If you don't think I have the skills necessary to perform the job, I'll leave. I can find work elsewhere." He planted his cowboy hat on his head and started for the door.

He'd spoken with such intensity and passion, he'd practically stolen Kalea's breath away. Suddenly, she didn't want the man to leave. A Navy SEAL? Wow. "Hawk," she called after him.

He stopped but didn't turn around.

"One more question." She waited until he faced her before she asked, "Why Hawaii?"

"I was with the Special Patrol Insertion/Extraction Training. We performed insertions and extractions over Maui, Kauai, Oahu and the Big Island of Hawaii. I spent a couple days on Hawaii. When I discovered there was one of the biggest and oldest cattle ranches in the U.S. on this island, I have to admit I was intrigued."

"How so?" Kalea asked.

"I grew up on a cattle ranch in Montana. I couldn't imagine anywhere but the Midwestern plains as a suitable place to raise a large herd. The idea that Hawaii had one of the most successful cattle ranches in the U.S. stunned me. I had to check it out." He spread his arms wide. "So, here I am."

Kalea wasn't sure she liked Hawk's response. It was too convenient.

"There you have it." Her father clapped his hands together. "Hawk starts tomorrow. I expect you to show him around the ranch and teach him everything you know. He'll be your shadow for the next couple of weeks."

"Weeks?" Kalea shook her head. "If he knows as much about ranching as he says he does, it will only take a day or two for him to come up to speed."

"I want him to be more than a *paniolo*," her father said. "Maleko is getting older. We need to consider grooming someone to take his place."

Kalea stared at her father in alarm. "Maleko isn't old. He'll be around for many more years to come."

Her father held up both hands. "I expect so, but it wouldn't hurt to start grooming someone to fill his shoes should he wish to take a vacation or time off for medical reasons."

Kalea's brow furrowed. "Do you know something I don't? Maleko isn't ill, is he? He'd tell me if he was, wouldn't he?"

Her father waved a hand. "Maleko is fine. Just do as I say and bring Hawk up to speed with everything you know. Now, if you'll excuse me, I have some calls to make before dinner. And you need to shower."

Having been dismissed, Kalea turned. "If you'll follow me, I'll show you to your room." Her father wanted the new *paniolo* in the blue room. The bedroom next to hers. Shadowing was one thing. Having the handsome cowboy in the room next to her was something else. She was not amused. And every time he touched her, she experienced an alarming shock of awareness that took her aback and confused her at the same time. Why did he have that effect on her? He was only a man.

Two weeks in his company sounded like an eternity. She'd give him two days and find a way to lose him. If he was all he said, he'd catch on quickly and cease to require unnecessary hand holding. And yet, the thought of holding Hawk's hand sent a delicious shiver across her skin...

Nope.

She didn't need that kind of distraction. Not now. Not when she needed to be fully aware of her surroundings and everything in them. She hadn't told her father there had been another attempt to kidnap her when she'd slipped away from one of her bodyguards to visit a sick friend in the town closest to the Parkman Ranch. She'd stopped at a grocery store after dark. Someone had come out of the shadows wearing a ski mask. She'd jumped into the truck before he'd reached her, and hit the door locks in the nick of time. Kalea hadn't notified the police because word would have gotten back to her father, and he would've locked her up for the rest of her life to keep her safe.

Kalea figured as long as she was at home on the ranch, she should be okay. When she left the ranch, she'd have to be more aware of her surroundings. She'd even ordered a can of mace to carry for when she was in Hilo or Waimea.

In the meantime, she'd have her shadow following her. She cast a glance at the new ranch hand. It might not be a bad thing that he was going to follow her around. He could watch her back. Not that she needed him to on the ranch, but it wouldn't hurt.

CHAPTER 3

Hawk fell in step beside Kalea as they left the study and climbed the staircase to the second floor.

He couldn't believe he'd been so wrong about this assignment. All the while he'd been in flight to Hawaii, and even up to the point he'd met his charge, he'd had it in his mind that she was a little girl. Not a grown woman, almost as old as he was.

As if that wasn't bad enough, she was drop-dead gorgeous, with her long, dark, wavy hair, big brown eyes and full, luscious lips. Even in jeans and a dirty shirt and smelling of horse and outdoors, her beauty was undeniable.

But then, Hawk had always appreciated the smell of horses and the outdoors. He'd missed the earthy scents of a barn and livestock when he'd been in the southern California city of San Diego. Here, in Hawaii of all places, he almost felt at home.

Kalea stopped on the landing and flung open a door to a room decorated in light gray-blue with wood accents. "You'll be in this room. I'm sorry to say, but it doesn't have a bathroom attached. You'll have to share the one down the hallway."

"After my time in the desert, I'm just happy to have running water. I'll survive."

"Dinner is in thirty minutes in the main dining room. You can explore and find your own way, if you like. Or, if you want to wait while I shower, I'll get you there."

"I'll find my own way." He'd use the time she was in the shower to look around the house and the surroundings to find all the weaknesses in security. He needed more time with her father to go over all the employees Kalea came into contact with on a daily basis. He'd have Hank's computer guy run background checks on them to see if any sent up red flags.

In the meantime, he'd get to know Kalea and stick to her like glue. He had a feeling the task would be more difficult than he'd anticipated. She had spunk and didn't seem the type to suffer fools or restrictions. Since she'd ditched her last two bodyguards, she had proven herself independent and resistant to someone following her every move.

Those bodyguards might have been good at protecting people willing to submit to their guidelines, but neither one of them could ride a horse. Thus, John Parkman's plea to Hank that he provide someone who was familiar with ranching and could ride a horse well enough to keep up with his daughter.

John had warned him that she would do everything in her power to lose him, if she knew he was there to protect her. She was stubborn and prized her independence.

With this being his first assignment with the Brotherhood Protectors, Hawk had to prove himself. He refused to fail. And if he could find out who was threatening Kalea and neutralize that threat, he might get back to Montana sooner.

He stood in the hallway as Kalea moved to the room beside his and entered. As she crossed the threshold, she shot a glance his way, a frown marring her pretty, dark brow.

If Hawk wasn't mistaken, Kalea wasn't happy about being stuck with him. Nor was she happy her father had assigned him to the room beside hers.

Hawk grinned her way. "Looking forward to working with you, Miss Parkman."

She frowned. "Call me Kalea."

"Yes, ma'am." He waved like a cowboy eager to start his first job and ducked into his room, leaving his door open just enough to hear footsteps in the hallway should Kalea decide to sneak past him.

Hawk spent a few short minutes organizing his gear, unpacking and setting out his toiletries kit. Used to a life of blow-and-go tactics, it didn't take him long, and he was back out in the hallway.

Kalea had just stepped out of her room, clothing in hand, crossing the hallway to the bathroom. She glanced his way, her eyes widening.

He gave her a mock salute, spun on a boot heel and headed for the stairs. Kalea would be busy in the shower long enough for him to ask John Parkman a few questions about the employees and layout of the ranch. He hadn't had enough time before Kalea had arrived earlier to get all the details, just confirmation that he was supposed to work undercover as a ranch hand.

John Parkman was still in his study, seated behind a massive mahogany desk with the door open.

Hawk knocked on the doorframe.

Mr. Parkman looked up. "Oh, Hawk, please, come in." He pushed back from the desk and walked around it, holding out his hand.

Hawk shook his new client's hand. "Sir, I have a few questions I'd like to get out of the way while Miss Parkman is otherwise occupied."

Parkman's gaze shot to the door.

"She's in the shower. Which probably gives us a few minutes."

"Five…max." Her father grinned. "She doesn't waste a lot of time. Not my girl."

Hawk filed that tidbit of information away in things-to-know-about-Kalea. "I'd like to get a list of all the employees of the Parkman Ranch and run background checks on them to see if any of them pop up as a potential threat."

Parkman's lips screwed up in a grimace. "There are over three hundred and fifty employees. That could take some time. We run each new hire through a screening process. I don't know that a background check will do you much good."

Three hundred and fifty employees? Wow. Hawk didn't blink an eye, even though he was shocked at the number of people it took to run the ranch. He hadn't read that number in the packet Hank had provided. "How about a list of people Miss Parkman is in contact with on a daily basis? That will narrow down the potential threats. My boss, Hank Patterson, has a computer guy who can tap into a number of data bases."

Parkman nodded. "I'll make a list and get it to you by tomorrow morning. Anything else you might need?"

Hawk nodded. "How did Miss Parkman slip by her previous bodyguards?"

John Parkman laughed. "None of them could ride a horse like my daughter. And they didn't know her favorite places on the ranch to hide. One in particular is in a copse of trees a couple miles out from the ranch house. There's a stream among the trees and a small waterfall. On a hot day, she likes to swim in the stream. You can locate the trail into the woods, if you find the tree with the four-foot high stump next to it. The path into the woods is to the right of the stump. That stump was a twin to the tree still standing until it was snapped by cyclone-force winds a few years back."

"I'll keep that in mind," Hawk said. "Although, I don't plan on letting her get that far ahead of me."

The older man snorted. "She's got one of the fastest horses in our stables."

"Then I'll need a faster horse," Hawk said.

"How long has it been since you've been riding?"

"The last time I was home in Montana a year ago. Riding isn't something you forget."

With a nod, Parkman said, "Ask Maleko for Pain Killer. He's faster than Kalea's horse. I have to warn you, though, he can be cantankerous and ornery. You have to show him who's boss up front."

"Roger." Hawk glanced at his watch. "I'd like to take a quick look around the exterior of the house before Miss Parkman is done in the shower. I'll be back inside in time for dinner."

Mr. Parkman held out his hand, his face grave. "Glad to have you on board. I'm worried my daughter's independence will cost her dearly. I can't lose Kalea. She's all I have."

Hawk gave Parkman a firm handshake. "Understood. I'll protect her with my life, if necessary."

"That's all I need to know." The older man's lips twisted. "Good luck keeping up with her. She's had free run of this ranch from the day she learned to walk. She knows it like the back of her hand." He lifted a photo off his desk. "Kalea's mother was pure indigenous Hawaiian. She passed when Kalea was a little girl. I promised I'd take care of Kalea. I love her with all my heart." He pressed a hand to his chest. "Sometimes, she looks so much like her mother, it hurts."

Hawk's chest tightened.

The loss of his wife obviously still grieved the older man.

Parkman waved toward the French doors on one side of the study. "Don't let me hold you up. You don't have much time to look around. You can leave through these doors."

Hawk stepped out onto the porch that wrapped around the sprawling ranch house. He studied the view, enjoying the lush green fields dotted with Charolais and a surprising backdrop of the Mauna Kea snow-capped mountain.

"Amazing, isn't it?" John Parkman joined him on the porch. "Did you know that mountain is the tallest mountain in the world?"

"I thought Mount Everest was," Hawk turned to look at the older man.

"It's a matter of perspective," Parkman said. "If you consider from base to peak, Mauna Kea is the tallest. You see, the base is almost twenty-thousand feet below the Pacific Ocean. The mountain extends more than thirteen thousand feet above sea level, making it over thirty-three thousand feet high. Mount Everest, in comparison, stands just over twenty-nine thousand feet above sea level."

"I did not know that. Thirteen thousand feet is impressive enough. I knew Hawaii had a tall mountain, but snow-capped peaks seem so incongruous against the green pastures and palm trees found around the coast." Hawk smiled. "Still, it kind of reminds me of home."

Mr. Parkman laid a hand on Hawk's shoulder. "This ranch has been home to my family since the early 1800s. We love the land and respect what it gives us."

"I can understand why," Hawk said. The pastures weren't all that different from the ones he knew in Montana. Perhaps they were a little greener and lusher, but cattle and horses grazed the land, and cowboys still wore jeans and cowboy hats. "If you'll excuse me, sir, I'll take a look around."

Parkman nodded and returned to his study.

Hawk circled the house, studying the entrances, the windows and access to the second floor where Kalea's room was located. A shadowy silhouette appeared in the window behind a thin white curtain. He couldn't make out the details of her face, but the shape of the body was all female from the curve of her hips to the swells of her breasts. When she turned sideways, the tips of her perky breasts were clearly outlined, causing a decided tug in Hawk's groin.

He dragged his gaze away from the window, chiding himself for being a gawking, peeping Tom. Kalea was his client. He wasn't there to fall for the cattle rancher's spoiled daughter. He was there to keep her safe. Hawk stuffed his hands in his pockets, reminding himself to keep them there and off the woman.

As he completed his circumference of the house, a bright white Lexus SUV pulled up in the driveway, and a beautiful, sophisticated blonde swung out her legs and emerged. She wore a gray pinstripe business suit jacket and matching skirt and a pair of black patent leather pumps with three-inch heels. Long, trim legs peeked out from beneath the narrow skirt, and a fair amount of cleavage was on display in the neckline of a filmy white blouse. She carried a black leather briefcase that probably cost more than Hawk's first paycheck as a Navy SEAL.

"Excuse me, are you looking for someone?" she asked as she walked with purpose toward the house.

"No, ma'am," Hawk replied. "Just looking."

"Then perhaps you should leave before I call 911. You're trespassing on private property." She stood with her head held so high she looked down her nose at Hawk as if he was something smelly on her expensive shoes.

Hawk usually gave people the benefit of a doubt before forming an opinion about them, but this woman rubbed him wrong from the get-go. "I was invited." He pinned a tight smile on his face. "Perhaps you're the one trespassing."

The woman's perfectly made up gray eyes narrowed. "Don't be rude."

He gave her a tight-lipped smile. "Not rude. Truthful." He raised his eyebrows. "Are you looking for someone?"

She snorted and started past him.

He shot an arm out, stopping her from reaching the porch.

"Well, I never—"

"—treated a stranger with kindness?" he finished for her. "Again, are you looking for someone?"

"Ah, Clarise," Mr. Parkman's booming voice sounded from the front door of the house. "I didn't expect you back until the morning. The marketing plan could have waited until then."

Clarise smiled up at Parkman. "John, darling, I said I'd get it to you as soon as possible. And this is the soonest." Her professionally whitened teeth gleamed in the dusk. Then she looked down her nose at Hawk. "John, is this...someone?"

Parkman chuckled. "Clarise Sanders, meet Hawk. He's our latest *paniolo* hire. He's fresh out of the military and ready to go to work here at Parkman Ranch."

She blinked and stood back as if he might give her cooties. "What is he doing at the house? Don't you have ranch hand quarters more suitable for your cowboys?"

Hawk fought to keep from rolling his eyes. The woman irritated the crap out of him, but not enough for him to sink as low as she was in her attitude and treatment of other employees of the Parkman Ranch conglomerate. He stood back and let her act the fool.

"Hawk is staying at the house. I've put Kalea in charge of training him, so I wanted him to be close by." The half-truth slid right off of John's tongue, though he shot a glance at Hawk during his explanation.

Hawk gave the slightest of nods, indicating his concurrence with the man to keep his real purpose under wraps.

"Well, can he sneak around somewhere else?" She glared at Hawk. "We have work to do."

John held out a hand to Clarise. "We have dinner on the table. Work can wait until after our meal. Would you care to join us?"

The woman's brow smoothed. "As a matter of fact, I worked straight through lunch. I'm famished. Thank you." She curled her hand into the crook of John's elbow and let him lead her into the house.

Hawk shook his head. The woman knew who to play up to, and a lowly cowboy wasn't it. Clarise couldn't take Kalea in a fight, and she certainly wouldn't want to break a nail. But she might know someone who could easily overpower a woman. He added her name to his mental list of people Patterson should run through a background check.

Quickly finishing his inspection of the outside of the house, Hawk made his way through the back door and found the dining room in time to be seated for dinner.

Mr. Parkman sat at the head of the table. Clarise took the seat to his left.

Hawk glanced around the room and looked toward the door. Kalea had yet to arrive. He stepped out into the foyer and looked up the sweeping staircase.

Kalea stood at the top, her hand on the rail. Her eyes flared when she spotted him, and she hesitated.

Hawk's breath caught and held.

Wearing a flowing white dress that hung down to mid-calf, she was stunning. Her dark complexion contrasted perfectly with the pure white of the dress. She'd left her hair hanging down her back in a long, wavy damp mass, reaching all the way past her waist. On her head, she wore a crown of pale pink and white plumeria. Unlike Clarise's three-inch high heels, Kalea wore flat-soled white sandals that laced up her ankles.

She floated down the stairs like a cloud, drifting toward him.

It took every one of those stairs before Hawk could pull himself together.

Her brow puckered. "Am I last?"

"No, ma'am," he said. "We both are." He held out his arm.

For a moment, she stared at his arm but finally tucked her hand into the bend of his elbow and allowed him to lead her into the dining room where her father and Clarise were already seated. All the way into the room, he caught whiffs of the fresh flowers in her hair and knew, forever after, he would always associate that scent with Kalea.

A hint of a frown appeared on Kalea's forehead when she first entered the room and spotted Clarise. But the frown disappeared and a smile replaced it when she turned to her father.

John Parkman stood and kissed his daughter on both cheeks. "Beautiful...just like your mother," he whispered.

Hawk held out her chair, seating her on the other side of her father, before taking the seat beside her.

The meal was served, starting with a salad topped with walnuts, dried cranberries and a vinaigrette. Next came a steak grilled to perfection with a side of asparagus and a sea-salt coated baked potato.

Hawk settled in for the wonderful meal, aware of the woman at his side's every move and word. The more he studied her, the more intrigued he became. How could someone who'd shown up earlier in dusty jeans and a cowboy boots transform into a beautiful Hawaiian beauty in a matter of minutes?

He figured he had his job cut out for him, if he hoped to keep up with the many sides of the rancher's daughter.

KALEA PICKED AT HER SALAD, choosing to eat the cranberries and walnuts. She'd never liked vinaigrette dressing but didn't want to hurt the chef's feelings. Ule had been on a kick to try different recipes, much to

John Parkman's dismay. As the steak was served, Kalea smiled.

Her father preferred meat and potatoes. Apparently, he'd gotten his way for the majority of the meal.

Kalea wanted to dig in, hungry after a hard day out on the ranch, but dressed as she was, she didn't feel right wolfing down her meal. Her mother's voice in her head made her sit with her hand in her lap, acting like a lady, not a ranch hand. Across from her, Clarise picked at her salad, and then pushed her steak around on her plate.

Fortunately, her father and Hawk had no qualms about eating beef. They polished off their meal, speaking very little until they'd consumed more than half the food on their plates.

Kalea forced herself to take smaller bites, relishing the flavors Ule had worked so hard to create. But by the time her father and Hawk had finished their food, she couldn't hold back any longer. To hell with the fancy dress. She was hungry!

"I would think after working with the animals as much as you do, you'd be less inclined to eat them," Clarise said, her steak still intact on her plate.

Kalea popped the last piece of her steak into her mouth and chewed without a comeback to the other woman's comment. She owed Clarise no explanation or apology for what she ate.

"My daughter likes what she does and what she eats," her father said. "And she works harder than most men." He winked at her. "Eat up, Kalea, you need to put some meat on your bones."

She sat back in her chair and smiled at her father for sticking up for her. "Ule did a great job on the meal."

"Yes, he did," Hawk said. "Was the steak from one of Parkman Ranch cattle?"

Her father's chest puffed out, proudly. "It's the only beef we eat around here."

"It's the only beef we want all Hawaiians to eat," Clarise said. "In fact, we want to expand our current exports to the contiguous forty-eight states and Alaska," Clarise said.

Kalea's father nodded. "I know. The marketing plan you wanted me to see."

"Yes, I wanted to go over the plan and a proposal for expanding our tourism trade. We've been approached about building a spa resort on the ranch."

Kalea stiffened. Clarise had been pushing for some time to expand the role of tourism on the ranch. Kalea didn't want more people wandering around than they already had.

"I'm not interested in expanding much beyond our current dude ranch experience," her father said. "We're primarily a cattle ranch, not a spa resort. I'd like to keep it that way."

"But, if you'll just look—"

"You're not going to change my mind, Clarise," he said, smiling as he shook his head.

Clarise pouted. "John, darling, you can be so stubborn."

He nodded. "Yes, I can, my dear. We'll discuss this— after dessert."

Ule entered the room. The older Hawaiian chef

frowned. "I didn't make a dessert. Miss Kalea insisted you didn't need a dessert."

Kalea cringed as her father turned a glare toward her. "You know what Dr. Brennen said. You need to cut back on your carbs. That huge potato you just ate contained more carbs than you need in a day, much less one meal."

"Damned quack doesn't know what he's talking about. I'm perfectly healthy."

"Except for high blood pressure and cholesterol." She reached out and touched his hand. "I'd like to keep you around a lot longer," she said softly.

Her father grimaced then tossed his cloth napkin onto his plate. "I guess that concludes our meal." He pushed back his chair and stood. "Clarise, if you want to show me that marketing plan, we can go over it in my study now."

"And no sneaking chocolates," Kalea said. "For that matter, I'll come with you." She followed her father and Clarise out of the dining room, shooting a glance over her shoulder at Hawk. "I'll see you at dawn tomorrow morning."

She'd rather have stayed and gotten to know the new *paniolo* better, but she didn't trust her father to keep his hand out of the chocolate he kept stashed in his desk.

Kalea sighed. She'd have all the next day to find out why Hawk had really come to Parkman Ranch. With all the skills of a Navy SEAL, it didn't seem right he'd come to be a cowboy on the massive ranch. Something smelled fishy, and she suspected it was the SEAL.

CHAPTER 4

FULL OF ONE of the best steaks he'd had in a long time, Hawk needed to walk off some of the calories he'd ingested. Since Kalea was occupied with her father, that left Hawk to wander around on his own. He stepped outside into the cool night breeze and stared up at the sky, brightly lit with billions of shiny stars. The night sky in this part of Hawaii was very much like the big sky of Montana. Far from city lights, he could see the Milky Way and a couple of the planets, gleaming in the heavens.

A horse's soft nickering drew his attention back to Earth and the nearby paddock. He loved horses but liked taking a treat with him when greeting the animals for the first time. Hawk ducked back into the house, found the kitchen and introduced himself to the chef.

"Hello, I'm Jace Hawkins, the new *paniolo*." He held out his hand to the man in the white apron.

Dark eyes narrowed as they looked him up and

down. "I'm Ule Kekoa, Mr. Parkman's personal chef." The man took his hand. "I hear you were a Navy SEAL."

"Yes, sir."

"I spent eight years in the Navy. It's where I learned to cook." He gave Hawk a firm handshake. "Thank you for your service."

"Thank you for yours. Our soldiers and sailors need fine cooks to keep us healthy and able to fight."

Ule waved a hand around the kitchen. "Is there anything I can do or get for you?"

"As a matter of fact, yes." Hawk smiled. "Could I get a carrot?"

"Of course," Ule said. "For you or a horse?"

Hawk chuckled, glad the chef understood the needs of a rancher. "For a horse."

Ule reached into a bin. "You'll find the horse carrots in this bin. Miss Kalea grabs a few every morning. I make sure to keep it stocked for her and the horses." He handed Hawk a long, orange carrot.

Hawk took the offering. "Mahalo."

The older man nodded, a smile tilting his mouth. "*Ho'omau.*"

"I'm sorry. My grasp of the Hawaiian language is limited to *aloha*, *mahalo* and *luau*," Hawk admitted.

"*Ho'omau* means persevere, keep going. Never give up." He straightened his shoulders and lifted his chin. "Our *ali'i* is strong-willed and stubborn. But her heart is kind, and her love for the people and her home is solid. Don't give up on her."

"I'm honored that's she's agreed to train me." Hawk

wondered why Ule had asked him not to give up on Kalea. Did he know the real reason Hawk was there? He left the house, stepped down from the porch and crossed the lawn to a split-rail fence. The sky full of stars created enough of a glow he didn't need to carry a flashlight.

A dark gelding trotted up to the railing, tossing its head and nickering softly.

Hawk held out his empty hand to see if the horse would come up to him.

The animal snorted and danced away.

Holding out his hand with the carrot, Hawk waited for the horse to reconsider.

Without hesitation, the gelding nuzzled the carrot with his lips and sank his teeth into the treat.

Hawk held onto the end as the rest was snapped off. He reached out and smoothed his hand along the animal's neck, inhaling the scent of the animal. It brought back many good memories of growing up on a ranch in Montana.

"You're spoiling my horse," a familiar voice said behind him.

He held out his hand with the other half of the carrot. "Would you prefer to do it?" Hawk turned as Kalea took the other half of the carrot and held it out in the flat of her palm to the horse.

"His name is *Pupule.*" Kalea lifted the edge of her skirt, climbed up to sit on the top rail and rubbed her horse's nose.

Hawk tried not to but couldn't help admiring her trim calves and a hint of thigh beneath the hiked-up hem of her dress. As his groin tightened, he cleared his throat. "Is that a Hawaiian name?"

"Not so much a name as a word that describes him." She smiled and scratched the horse behind the ear. "It means crazy or insane."

Hawk laughed. "I'm afraid to ask…does he live up to his name?"

Kalea leaned her forehead against *Pupule's* head. "He was a spirited colt, dancing around the pasture for no apparent reason. Some thought he was crazy. It took me many months of work to calm him enough to ride."

"And now?" Hawk asked softly, enjoying watching her with the horse. The two had a special bond.

"He's the best horse I've ever owned. He knows what I want even before I do." She patted the horse's nose and started to lean away from the fence as if to jump to the ground. Her dress caught, and she would have ripped it, but Hawk reached out and grabbed her around the waist before her hip left the rail.

With a quick tug, she had her dress free.

Hawk let her slide down his front until her feet touched the ground. For a moment, he continued to hold her, his hands resting on her hips. "Are you okay?"

She stared up into his face, her eyes rounded. Then she nodded and stepped away. "Thank you. I tear more dresses than any woman I know."

"I'm sure they aren't made for climbing onto fence rails." He reached out and patted the horse's nose. "But *Pupule* doesn't seem to care."

"That's what I like about him. He's the only male I

know who appreciates me no matter what I wear." She snorted softly. "As long as I bring him carrots."

"I'm sure it's more than the carrots," Hawk murmured.

She cleared her throat then looked upward. "Are the skies this clear and bright in Montana?" Kalea asked.

"Yes, they are," Hawk's gaze shifted from the sky to the woman beside him.

She was a contradiction of personalities in one person. The tough as nails rancher he'd first met that afternoon and the soft and feminine Hawaiian beauty standing beside him. He didn't know which one was the true Kalea, but he suspected she was both.

"Have you ever lived anywhere else but Hawaii?" he asked.

She nodded. "I attended college in San Diego." Her lips quirked upward on the edges. "Not far from where the Navy SEALs train. I remember one of my friends had a brother who was a Navy SEAL. I was in awe of how strong and brave they were."

"It's strange to think we might have been in San Diego at the same time."

"Only a few miles apart." She shook her head. "And we never knew each other existed. We had to come all the way to Hawaii to meet."

"I've learned over the years in the military that this is a great big world. At the same time, it can seem so small. I've run into people I know in the most out of the way places."

"And now, you're in Hawaii," Kalea whispered. "Not

many people ever make it outside the borders of their own state."

"I'm not one of them."

"Obviously."

Though she'd moved out of his arms, Kalea still stood close enough that the scent of plumeria teased his nostrils.

Apparently, the flowers in Kalea's hair tempted *Pupule* as well. He reached over the top of the fence and tried to get a bite of her flowery crown.

"Hey!" Kalea laughed and moved out of range. "Those aren't for you." Pulling the crown of flowers from her hair, she held it in her hand.

Her smile and laughter touched a part of Hawk he hadn't known was lost until that time, making him all the more determined to see Kalea safe from harm.

Holding her in his arms, even for that brief moment had made him want to hold her again. That wasn't a good idea. He was pretty sure being a bodyguard meant remaining emotionally detached from the subject he was to guard. Getting involved with the pretty Hawaiian would distract him from his ultimate purpose. That couldn't happen. She was the job. Her father was counting on him. Her life depended on Hawk's ability to protect her.

He had to maintain focus. Which meant...

Hands. Off.

KALEA'S HEART beat so fast she was certain she wasn't getting enough oxygen to her brain. Especially when her brain was telling her how good it had felt being in Hawk's arms. Yes, the blood was either carrying too little oxygen or not enough. Whichever way made for scrambled brain cells.

Jace Hawkins wasn't a man to be fooled with. Not that she was interested in fooling around with the man. If he was truly a *paniolo*, he was off limits. He worked for the ranch, which meant he was an employee. Kalea didn't flirt with employees. It was strictly forbidden.

If he was a bodyguard, he was still an employee of her father and the ranch. Again, Kalea didn't flirt with employees.

Then why was her heart racing and a swarm of butterflies beating against the insides of her belly? So, he'd helped her down from the fence with his big hands encircling her waist. She'd felt their warmth through the thin layer of her dress's fabric. It made her want to feel his hands against her naked skin.

Impossible. She was back to the principal edict. You don't screw around with employees.

Kalea drew in a deep breath, telling herself she needed to walk away. She should leave Hawk and go to her room where she would sleep the night. A night filled with thoughts of him lying in the room beside her, plaguing her sleep and keeping her awake into the wee hours of the morning wondering if he slept in pajamas or in the nude. She bet he slept nude.

Immediately, her mouth dried, and she found it difficult to swallow.

Why was her mind going to places it hadn't gone before? Sure, she wasn't a virgin. She'd experimented with sex when she was in college, away from the ranch and the small-town atmosphere of her home. But it hadn't been all it was advertised.

Or maybe she hadn't met the man who could set her body on fire. With only a touch, Hawk had managed to make her blood burn through her veins like the molten lava of the Kilauea volcano. How was she going to get through the night with him in the room beside her? And then she had to spend the next days, weeks, or more, training him in the ways of the Parkman Ranch.

No. No. No.

If it got to be impossible, she'd lose him, damn it. She'd lost all the previous men her father had saddled her with. If he was only a cowboy learning about the ranch and his teacher ditched him, he'd head back to the barn and ask Maleko what he could do to help until his instructor returned. If he truly was another attempt by her father to provide her with a bodyguard, he'd continue to look for her. She'd flush him out the next day. One way or another.

In the meantime, she had to get through the night with the heat of his hands still tingling at her waist.

"I'm headed to bed," she said and started for the house. "Please, don't feel like you have to follow. The night is too nice to ignore." She hoped he'd stay outside until she made it into the house and up to her room. The more she was with him, the weaker her resistance grew.

Kalea prided herself in her strength and independence. She wouldn't let any man derail her in either. Not intentionally. Not even if she liked it when he lifted her off a fence and let her slide down his body to the ground.

She had turned and hurried toward the house, wondering if he'd find it strange if she broke into a sprint.

At first, she thought he'd taken her up on enjoying the night sky without her. Seconds after she'd turned away and started for the house, he appeared beside her, his footsteps silent against the cushion of grass.

Kalea's jaw clamped down hard to keep from telling him to bug off and leave her alone. If she was honest with herself, she was glad he'd followed her. Though she knew it was safer if he hadn't, she couldn't deny the unwarranted attraction she felt toward the man. Was it because he'd been a Navy SEAL? Probably. Time spent in San Diego attending college had made her fully aware of the SEAL training. She and her girlfriends had gone to a party where the SEALs had been. Kalea had been so impressed she'd been tongue-tied.

And now, she had one beside her. Broad chest, thick, muscular thighs and a smile that made her panties damp. All of these things equaled a recipe for disaster. Even if the man wasn't an employee of the ranch, he couldn't possibly wish to live in Hawaii for the rest of his life. He'd been to many places in the world. After moving around so much, how could a man stay still?

Don't get ahead of yourself, she chided internally. They'd only just met. It wasn't as if he was a candidate for love ever after. He might even have a wife or girl-friend back Stateside, though she couldn't image any

43

woman letting this man out of her sight for more than a day.

"I didn't ask, but do you have family joining you soon?" As soon as the words were out of her mouth, she wished she could withdraw them. "I'm not trying to be nosy. I mean, I need to know whether you'll need a larger room or one of the small cottages on the ranch to live in." Now, she was babbling.

"No," he said. "As a Navy SEAL, I didn't feel it was fair to have a family I'd never see. It was another reason I chose to leave the service. I couldn't set down roots until I knew I'd be home more than a few weeks out of the year."

Kalea let go of the breath she hadn't realized she'd been holding. "That's good," she said, and again, wished she hadn't. "Not...good...that you don't have a family, but that your current sleeping arrangements will suffice." In the room beside hers. Just one room over, he could be lying in the bed naked. Her core heated. She picked up the pace until she was just short of jogging.

"Are you in a hurry to get to bed?" Hawk asked, easily keeping up with her. His legs and stride were longer than hers.

While Kalea was almost breathing hard, he walked with ease.

When they reached the door, he opened it and held it for her as she passed through, brushing against his arm as she did.

That blast of electricity ripped through her again. She shot a glance toward him and caught a slight frown denting his brow. Had he felt it, too?

Kalea couldn't get up the stairs fast enough. She started up the grand staircase.

"I'm going to the kitchen. Do you need anything before you turn in?" he asked from behind her.

Kalea halted so fast she almost fell over the step in front of her. So, he wasn't going to follow her all the way to her room. Thank goodness. She breathed a sigh of relief, which was quickly followed by a strange niggle of disappointment. What had she expected? If he followed her, they'd part ways in front of their respective doors. It wasn't as if he'd ask to join her in her room or in her bed.

Her cheeks heated at the thought. "No...No...I'm fine. I'll see you at sunup. There are some cattle in one of the fields a couple miles out from the ranch. I'd like to get an early start."

"Yes, ma'am." He gave her a mock salute and a grin.

"Seriously, don't call me ma'am. It makes me feel old." She shook her head. "Everyone calls me Kalea."

"Some call you *ali'i*. What does that mean?"

Her cheeks burned. "Nothing. Just a term of endearment. Goodnight." She turned and hurried up the stairs.

Great. Now he'd know the older employees who'd known her since she was a baby called her princess. She'd worked hard over the years to prove to them she wasn't a worthless drain on the ranch. Everything she did was to help improve the land, the animals and the lives of the people who worked the land and the surrounding community.

Why it bothered her that Hawk might know they called her princess was beyond her comprehension.

What he thought of her didn't matter. She had nothing to prove to him. Besides, he wouldn't be around for long, if she had her way. Either he'd keep up, or her father would assign someone else to train him. Kalea didn't have time to babysit a new employee. And she didn't need a bodyguard. There hadn't been another incident since the first. She suspected it had been a crime of chance and circumstance more than a premeditated attempt to capture or hurt her.

She'd been fortunate that she'd been paying attention when she'd been accosted in the city of Hilo. When a guy had come at her, wearing a Phantom of the Opera face mask, Kalea had been walking across the parking lot of a hardware store, a heavy bag of fence nails in her hand.

The man had run at her, full tilt.

Kalea, acting on pure self-preservation instinct, had swung the bag as hard as she could.

He'd raised his hand to block the blow, but too late.

She'd hit him in the side of the head.

He'd spun away, clutching at his injured face. That's when she'd seen the snake tattoo on the back of his hand. By the time he'd turned back to her, he'd missed his opportunity.

Kalea had run back into the store and asked for assistance.

By the time the store manager came out with her to her truck, the man had disappeared.

Kalea had felt stupid and wondered if she'd perhaps imagined the man in the mask.

Unfortunately, the store manager knew her father

and had called him to ask how she was. That had set her father to thinking that the person who'd attacked her knew who she was and wanted her for the potential ransom her father would pay to get her back alive.

Kalea counted it off as someone who'd found a lone woman in a parking lot and made his move.

That was, until it happened again in Waimea, the small town near the ranch. Other women had been in and out of the grocery store. Why would someone go specifically after her and not the others? Unless he knew who she was and what ransom her father would be willing to pay to get her back alive.

At first, Kalea had been leery of returning to town alone. But when her can of mace had come in the mail, she'd slipped it into her purse and felt a lot more confident. It wasn't a bag of nails, but she could shoot it before her attacker got close enough to grab her. She didn't need no stinkin' bodyguard. She could take care of herself.

Kalea stripped out of the pretty white dress, questioning her reasoning for wearing the dress for the first time that night. Had she secretly hoped to impress the new *paniolo*? To show him that she indeed wasn't just a cowhand, smelling of horse manure and dust?

Pulling a baggy T-shirt over her head, she stared at herself in the mirror. Her image was nothing like the sophisticated woman in the white dress of a few minutes ago. She appeared to be a girl-child in a T-shirt far too big for her. The hem hung down almost to her knees. Far from sexy.

Good.

She didn't need to be sexy to get some sleep. Tomorrow would be a busy day of testing the new hire and figuring out whether he was really a ranch hand or a bodyguard.

Kalea's gut screamed the man was a bodyguard. At the same time, low in her belly, her insides melted, a small voice telling her Hawk could guard her body anytime. As long as they were both naked when he was guarding her.

She threw herself on the mattress and hugged a pillow to her chest. Now, she was sure to be awake all night, thinking of a naked bodyguard in the room beside hers.

CHAPTER 5

AFTER A CRAPPY NIGHT'S SLEEP, Hawk rose before the crack of dawn, dressed in worn jeans, equally worn boots and a faded chambray shirt. The fancy boots, shirt and pressed jeans had been for meeting the client. A real cowboy didn't wear his best clothes to take care of horses and cattle. He wore something durable and comfortable. Something he could work in all day and sleep in at night, if he ended up out on the range after dusk when the sun set, and an animal needed to be watched through the night.

Plunking his cowboy hat on his head, he descended the stairs to the ground floor and went in search of coffee.

Ule was in the kitchen, already at work preparing breakfast for the household. Without a word, he pointed to the coffee pot and the mugs sitting on the counter beside it.

Thankful he didn't have to keep up his end of small talk, Hawk poured a cup of the steaming, rich brew.

He took it black. No sugar or cream.

"Good?" Ule asked.

"Perfect," Hawk replied. He watched as the Hawaiian cracked eggs into the skillet and set it on the gas burner.

After a couple fortifying sips of the tasty brew, Hawk set his mug on the counter, grabbed cutlery from a drawer and headed toward the dining room.

"We have breakfast in the kitchen," Ule called out.

Hawk changed directions and laid out the silverware on the large kitchen table. As he did, he frowned. "Is there a certain order I'm supposed to lay out the silverware?"

Ule shrugged. "Mr. Parkman never cares. Now, if Miss Clarise were coming to dinner, I would instruct you on proper dinnerware etiquette. She likes to think she knows best."

"What relationship is she to the Parkman family?"

Ule snorted. "If she had her way, she would be Mrs. Parkman."

"Is Mr. Parkman amenable to the idea?" Hawk asked.

Again, Ule shrugged. "She's pretty, in her high-falutin' ways. Hard for a man to ignore."

Wanting to marry a man, and his actually asking, were two very different things. Before he left for the field that day, Hawk needed to check in with Patterson, giving him what little information he had for the man to perform cyber investigation on some of the people who worked on the ranch.

A woman interested in marrying a wealthy landowner might think his daughter stood in the way of her goal. Though Parkman had conducted background checks on his employees, Hawk doubted the man did more than check on their criminal history. Patterson and his team of Brotherhood Protectors had other information they could tap into. Financial information said a lot about the stability of a person and his or her ability to think toward the future. If the bank account remained empty and the person lived from paycheck to paycheck, that might be enough motivation to make them want to kidnap someone for ransom. Or if someone in the family was sick, the motivation to earn more money outside of a regular paycheck would be high. Medical bills could pile up, providing additional stress.

Ule scraped scrambled eggs from a skillet into a large bowl and handed it to Hawk.

He carried it to the table and was setting it in the middle when Kalea appeared, dressed in jeans, boots, a faded pink blouse and carrying a cowboy hat. She had her dark hair pulled back in a long, thick braid. She looked far younger than her almost thirty years.

She frowned when she saw him with the bowl in his hand. "How long have you been up?"

"A little while." He turned to Ule, who handed him a plate of toast. He took it and set it in the middle of the table.

Ule followed with a platter of bacon, sausage and ham slices.

Mr. Parkman entered the room. "Smells good, Ule."

"Just hold off on the bacon and sausage," Kalea warned her father. "You know what your heart doctor said."

"A little bacon and sausage won't kill me."

She crossed her arms over her chest. "Not according to Dr. Adams."

Ule returned to the stove and brought back a bowl of steaming oatmeal.

Kalea smiled. "That's more like it.

Her father's frown made Hawk smother a chuckle.

Kalea patted the older man's arm. "I'm not trying to be mean. I want you to be around for a long time. Clogging your arteries won't achieve that goal." She leaned up on her toes and pressed a kiss to his cheek. "I love you, Dad."

He hugged her close. "Love you, too, sweetheart."

Hawk could feel the love between the father and daughter. It made him all the more determined to keep them safe from whomever was trying to hurt Kalea.

"There's enough food on this table to feed an army." Kalea shook her head and took a seat.

"You need to eat a good breakfast, Miss Kalea. You rarely eat lunch, and you work really hard," Ule said.

Mr. Parkman sat at the end of the kitchen table. "What's your plan for the day?"

Kalea scooped fluffy yellow scrambled eggs onto her plate. "I want to see if our new *paniolo* is as good as he says he is."

Hawk's hand froze for a brief moment halfway to the platter of bacon and sausage. Schooling his face to poker straightness, he continued in his pursuit of bacon. "What did you have in mind?"

"Nothing drastic. I'm riding out to the north forty to check on some of the cows due to calf. We'll save the guest cabins and dude ranch operations for another day. They're a few miles south of here and run by Keli'i Palakiki, our guest operations manager."

Her father chuckled and glanced across the table at Hawk. "How long did you say it's been since you've been riding?"

"A year," Hawk admitted. "I know where you're going with this. I don't doubt my ability to ride, but you're right. I'll be saddle sore the first couple of days." He shrugged. "The only way to get over it is to get on with it."

Kalea's lips twitched. "Can you be ready in fifteen minutes?"

He nodded and went to work cleaning his plate of food. Once he was done, he excused himself, ran up to brush his teeth and was back out in the barnyard in less than ten minutes.

Kalea was in the barn slinging a saddle over her horse's back.

Maleko had a gray appaloosa tied to a post. He gave Hawk a nod. "Mr. Parkman said you wanted to ride Pain Killer. We call him PK for short."

The gelding was steel gray except for white stockings and white hindquarters speckled with spots of black.

PK pulled at the lead rope, trying to catch a glimpse of Hawk. He pawed at the ground and tossed his head, as if to say, *Bring on your best.*

Having ridden broncs in the rodeo, Hawk knew he could hold his own. And if he was tossed from the back of the beautiful animal, he'd get back up in the saddle and show PK he wasn't afraid.

Apprehensive...but not afraid. Hell, he wasn't getting any younger at thirty-three years old.

Maleko handed Hawk a brush and disappeared into a tack room.

Hawk smoothed the brush over the horse's body, neck and belly.

By the time Maleko returned with a saddle blanket and saddle, Hawk had the horse shining and calm. He laid the blanket over the animal's back and settled the saddle over the blanket. When he tightened the cinch, PK puffed out his belly.

Hawk left the stirrup up and fit the bridle over the horse's nose and slipped the bit between his teeth. After he had the straps in place, he returned to the leather strap around PK's belly and tightened it another two inches. He wasn't a green cowboy who didn't know the saddle would be too loose once he'd gotten out of the barnyard. He adjusted the stirrups to a length that would fit his legs and led the horse out into the yard.

Kalea was already outside, mounted and heading for the gate to a pasture. She wasn't going to wait on him. If he wanted to learn about the Parkman Ranch and what his duties would be, he had to keep up.

Hawk stuck the toe of his boot into the stirrup. As he swung his leg over the saddle, PK spun around. He was ready, holding onto to the saddle horn until his leg was completely over and he sat hard on the saddle. Once he had both feet in the stirrups, he felt at home.

Yeah, he'd be sore after a day's riding, but being back in the saddle was where he'd longed to be.

So, it wasn't Montana. The lush pastures and blue skies of Hawaii were beautiful, and the powerful muscles of the horse beneath him promised to be a challenge he was prepared for.

Kalea leaned down to unlatch the gate, walked her horse through and paused briefly on the other side. She didn't walk away, leaving the gate open. Other animals could get through if she did that. No, she had the sense of a cowgirl. No matter how confined she might feel about leading the new hand around, she wasn't going to risk losing or injuring animals just because she was irritated.

Hawk gave PK a gentle nudge with his heels. The gelding leaped forward, nearly leaving Hawk behind. If he hadn't been as skilled as he was in the saddle, he would have been left sitting on the ground.

Instead, he leaned forward and breezed past Kalea.

The ranch owner's daughter closed and latched the gate. Then she took off at a trot across the pasture.

Hawk followed, urging PK to keep up.

Challenged by a horse in front of him, PK picked up speed and galloped after Kalea and *Pupule*.

Soon both horses ran neck-and-neck, one trying to get ahead of the other.

Hawk let PK have his head, the wind in their hair, the ground a blur beneath them.

As they approached another gate, Kalea slowed her horse to a trot then a walk.

Hawk did the same.

Kalea shot a glance toward him, her hair windblown and beautiful, her eyes shining bright. "So, *paniolo*, you can ride." She gave him a brief, approving nod. "Perhaps you can get the gate, this time."

Hawk nudged his horse forward, leaned down and unlatched the gate. PK danced backward. In order to hold the gate open, Hawk had to dismount. When he did, PK jerked his head high and pulled backward, slipping his reins free of Hawk's grip. Caught between holding the gate for Kalea and catching his horse, Hawk held the gate.

Kalea and her horse moved through the opening, PK lunged, pushing past Kalea and her mount, and raced back toward the barn and house, which had been out of sight for the past fifteen minutes.

Kalea laughed out loud. "You might as well start walking. It takes a while to get back to the barn on foot." Her laughter followed her as she rode away, leaving him standing there, without a horse and without his body to guard.

"Damn."

PK had already disappeared over a hill, heading back to the barn.

Kalea was moving at a trot, quickly putting distance between them.

After promising her father that he'd take care of Kalea, Hawk couldn't go back to the barn. That would leave Kalea unprotected for far too long. The only choice he really had was to follow Kalea and hope he could catch up with her sooner than later.

CHAPTER 6

THE FARTHER KALEA rode away from Hawk, the tighter her chest grew. She felt bad. Really bad, for leaving him standing out in the middle of the ranch, with no other way to get back to the barn than to walk. Had it been her father, Maleko or any other ranch hand, she'd have offered to let him climb on the back of her horse and given him a ride back.

Then why had she left Hawk?

Because she felt uncomfortable around him. Not in a creepy way. More in a want-to-get-naked-with-him way. She'd never met a man who had affected her in such a way within hours of meeting him.

She'd lain awake well into the night with the tingling sensation he'd caused when he'd wrapped his hands around her waist and lifted her off the fence as if she weighed next to nothing. Having grown up on the ranch, Kalea prided herself in being capable of doing anything a man could do and doing it better. In that one move of lifting her off the fence, Hawk had torn down her man-walls and revealed the woman behind them.

He'd made her feel feminine, vulnerable and desirable all in that moment. She thought she was mad but, in reality, she'd been scared at her own reaction to sliding down his chest until her feet hit the ground.

While she wanted to turn back and do what was right, her body burned at the thought of having Hawk riding behind her, his arms wrapped around her waist, his chest pressed to her back. The more she thought about it, the hotter she grew. Urging her horse to go faster, she steered him toward the one place on the ranch she loved most. Soon, she turned onto the trail beneath a canopy of trees, leading to her favorite creek and the pool of water where her mother and father had taught her to swim. As an adult, she came here when she needed to think. Something about the sound of the waterfall at the far end of the pool soothed her mind and soul.

She'd come here when her mother died. The waterfall had cried with her. When she'd finished crying, she'd entered the water and swum until her tears were washed away. She'd felt closer to her mother, who'd loved this place as much as she.

With her heart beating too fast and her thoughts tumbling over and over her unsettled feelings for the new *paniolo*, she dismounted and tied *Pupule* to a bush.

As always, the pool stretched out before her, the water smooth but for the ripple caused by the little waterfall. Sun found its way through the trees in bright spots dappling the water's surface.

Having left Hawk to walk home alone and still hot from her ride and her thoughts, Kalea pulled off her boots and socks, rolled up her jeans and waded in.

The cool liquid felt good against the skin of her feet and ankles.

Kalea closed her eyes and inhaled the scents of the trees, plants and water, willing the sound of the waterfall to soothe her thoughts and cool her heated body.

Inhale…exhale…inhale…

Her chest rose and fell with each breath. An image of Hawk standing at the gate, horseless and alone, intruded on her meditation.

Guilt gnawed at her gut.

Then an image of him standing in the moonlight looking up at her where she sat on the fence flooded her memory and her core heated.

Damn the man.

Though her feet were cool, the rest of her body lit up like the 4th of July. Her core heated and coiled inside.

The warmth of the air around her didn't help to tamp down the fire building deep in her loins.

Stepping out of the water, she unbuckled her belt and unzipped her jeans. She cast a quick glance around and laughed at herself. Even if he had followed her, Hawk wouldn't have caught up to her by now. Besides, he wouldn't know where to find her. She was completely alone.

Kalea shucked her jeans, her shirt, her bra and panties, and stacked them neatly on the branches of a bush. She pulled out the elastic band that held her ponytail, rearranged it to hold her hair up in a messy bun on top of her head, and slid into the water.

"Ahh," she murmured as she slowly swam across the pool to the waterfall on the other end. She'd been skinny-dipping in the pool since she'd been a young teen. Her father hadn't wanted her to be there alone, but she'd escaped there often. She'd learned early on to strip out of all of her clothes, swim naked, dry in the sun, redress in her clothes and return to the house with no one the wiser.

This was her oasis, the place that gave her a sense of peace she could find nowhere else on the ranch. Only this time, as she swam across the water, the water was cooling but the peace was elusive. Hawk's image would not shake free of her mind. His ruggedly handsome face with his gorgeous green eyes stared at her in her memory, reminding her she'd left him to walk several miles back to the house and barn. What if he got lost?

No, he couldn't get lost. The fields were wide open with few trees to disorient him. But what if he did get lost?

He'd eventually run into a fence and follow it to a junction...and walk a lot farther than he would have had to if he'd known the way.

Kalea reached the waterfall and stood under the spray, letting the water wash over her head and shoulders. No matter how long she stood there, the falling water didn't wash away her guilt or the nagging worry that Hawk could get lost and spend a lot of time wandering around the endless pastures.

"He's a Navy SEAL," she said out loud. "He's been

through a lot worse in BUD/S training. A long walk won't hurt him.

She lifted her face to the water and let it run over her eyes, her cheeks and mouth.

What would it feel like to stand beneath the waterfall with Hawk naked beside her?

She moaned. Why did she have to go there? The purpose of coming to the pool was to cleanse her heart, mind and soul of troubling thoughts, not make them worse.

Giving up on the waterfall, she lay on her back, staring up at the interlacing branches of the trees shading the grotto. Shafts of sunlight found cracks in the canopy and shone down into her eyes.

Kalea blinked and closed her eyes to the brightness. She floated in the pool, her ears beneath the water, her face in the sun, but the peace she sought proved more tenuous than in past visits.

Just when she was about to give up and go back to find Hawk, the water around her exploded in a loud splash, rocking her on a wave that sent her under.

Kalea sucked water into her nose and came up sputtering and gasping for air. Her first thought was of an earthquake, possibly brought on by another eruption of the volcano, Kilauea, on the other end of the Big Island.

Then the water parted beside her as a dark head surfaced.

Kalea squealed and backpaddled.

When the face cleared the surface with a broad grin, her squeal turned angry. "What the hell, Hawk?"

His grin broadened. "What a wonderful place. Why

didn't you tell me we were going to go for a dip? Is this something all the ranch hands get to do on their first day at Parkman Ranch?"

Kalea splashed water in his face. "You scared ten years off my life."

"Really?" His eyes widened...all innocence.

With a snort, she treaded water with one hand while she used her other arm to cover her breasts. She prayed the water was murkier lower down. Hell, he'd jumped in while she'd been floating on her back. He had to have seen everything.

Mortified, her cheeks burned. "How long have you been here?"

His lips curled. "Not long."

"Why didn't you head back to the barn, like I told you?"

He frowned. "I didn't figure I'd learn anything on the walk back, so I decided to follow you. And boy, am I glad I did. This place is great." He tipped his head back, allowing his body to rise to the surface.

And he was completely naked!

Kalea forgot to move her arms in the water and sank below the surface. She came up coughing.

Hawk was beside her in a second, his hands on her arms, pulling her up to the surface and to a shallower position where her feet could touch the ground. "Are you okay, Miss Parkman?"

She coughed. "No, I'm not okay. You're naked."

He looked at her with a confused frown. "And?"

She shook her head. "You're naked," she repeated,

unable to think of other words that would go along with her shocking discovery.

"In case you haven't noticed," he said, "so are you. I was just following your example."

"Yeah, but this is my spot. My pool. No one comes here but me."

"Oh," he said, his eyes wide with what appeared to be feigned regret and embarrassment.

"I thought you were showing me yet another perk of working on Parkman Ranch. But if my being naked embarrasses you, I'll get out." He started for the shore. With each step, his body rose further out of the water until his butt crack appeared at the surface.

"Wait!" Kalea yelled.

He started to turn.

Kalea should have closed her eyes, but she couldn't.

Then he was facing her, in all his incredibly muscular, sexy glory.

Her breath lodged in her lungs. She had no air to push words past her vocal cords. Not that her mind could engage to form a single coherent thought.

"Yes?"

Yes, yes, yes. Oh, man, yes!

Kalea opened her mouth, forming the word *yes*, when her mind kicked back in. She clamped her lips shut, physically shook herself and then said, "You didn't go back to the barn because you're another one of my father's bodyguards."

He stood still for a long moment, that impressive poker face in place.

"I knew it!" Kalea embraced the anger bubbling up inside, glad for the distraction over the blast of lust of a moment before. "Had you been a cowboy like my father painted you out to be, you would have gone after the horse. But no, you followed me. Because *I'm* the job…the client…the real reason you're here on Parkman Ranch."

Hawk reentered the water until it was up to his waist. "Your father loves you, and he's afraid for your life."

He kept coming toward her.

Her anger slipped a notch the closer he moved, replaced with that awe and lust of a moment before.

Though his man parts were submerged, she couldn't get the image of them out of her mind. Her blood hummed through her veins, sending heat to her core.

When he stopped in front of her, she backed up, sinking deeper into the pool until her nose was barely above the water.

Hawk gripped her arms and brought her back to stand in water only up to her chin. "If you're being targeted, don't you think it's a good idea to have someone watching your back? On the Navy SEAL team, we all looked out for each other. We knew no man could survive on his own."

"I'm not in the Navy, nor am I a SEAL," she said, her voice sounding breathy and completely unlike her normal confident tone.

"No, you're not. All the more reason to let me have your six." He stared down into her eyes. "At least, let me do my job. I have people who can help us find out who's doing this. Once we figure it out, we can put a stop to it.

When you're safe again, you can choose to send me back to the mainland. I'll be out of your hair, and you can carry on with your life as you see fit."

Sizzling synapses raced from where his fingers curled around her arms throughout her body. She could barely think past the fact they were naked in the water together, almost close enough for their private parts to touch. All she had to do was move a fraction of an inch closer…

She sucked in a deep breath, drawing on the little bit of control she could muster and lifted her chin. "I don't need a babysitter."

"No, you don't." His lips curled in a sexy smile. "You're a fully grown, beautiful woman. But you need an extra set of eyes in the back of your head if you're going to go it alone. Let me be that set of eyes. I might not be familiar with Hawaii and the Parkman Ranch, but I know my way around horses, and I'm trained in combat skills that could come in handy should you be attacked again." His hands slipped from her arms down to her hands. He lifted them up in his. "Please, let me help you."

Her heart pounded against her ribs, and her breasts tingled at the thought of rubbing up against his bare chest. How could she think when she was so close to all that…that…manliness?

"Okay," she blurted. So much for thinking. She looked down at where their hands were clasped together. She couldn't continue to look him in the eye without falling deeper into his gaze and getting lost in the mire of her muddled thoughts. "You can keep your job. But now that we both know you're a bodyguard, we can drop all pretense of training you as a *paniolo*."

He hesitated, his hands tightening on hers. "That might not be a good idea. The only people who know why I'm here are you, me and your father. The attacker doesn't know. As long as he thinks I'm just a hired hand, he might not consider me a threat or hindrance to getting to you."

Kalea's brows drew together. "I'm not so sure." She loved the way her hands felt so small enclosed his big, strong grip. What was she saying? Oh, yeah. "We made no secret that you're a former Navy SEAL."

"True." His thumb rubbed circles against the inside of her palm.

"I have other commitments that will take me away from the ranch that wouldn't make sense for a *paniolo* to tag along with me."

"You make a good point," he said, his voice deep, resonant and just a bit on the gravelly side.

It sent shivers across her naked, water-soaked skin.

"How about this..." he said. "We could make people think we're becoming a couple. That would explain our desire to be with each other at all times."

Her core coiled at his words *couple* and *desire*. His hands were close enough to her breasts, all she had to do was inhale deeply, and they'd come into contact.

What was wrong with her? She never lost control like she was at that moment, standing there in front of her bodyguard. She blinked several times, trying to focus her thoughts. As long as he held her hands in his and stood so close, she couldn't begin to make sense of anything.

With a strange sense of regret, she tugged her hands free of his and pushed back into the deeper water. "Let me think about this," she said, turned and swam away.

If she agreed to play the couple card, she'd have to be with him pretty much twenty-four-seven. Now that she'd seen all of him, could she even hope to keep it purely professional and hands-off? Hell, he worked for the Parkman Ranch. She had no choice. He was an employee. Which automatically meant keeping a professional distance.

Kalea swam around the pool in a slow breaststroke, her mind racing her, body no less heated than when she'd first entered the water. "If I agree to this, we're on a purely professional basis."

"Yes, ma'am."

"I make it a point not to date employees of the ranch."

"Have you told anyone of your position on dating?"

She turned and tread water. "No. It's just one of my values I've always lived up to."

He shrugged. "As long as you haven't made it known to others, it won't be a problem."

Not to the other members of the Parkman Ranch team, but to Kalea, it was an issue she'd have to live with.

"If we're going to pull it off, we have to show some PDA," Hawk said, his lip pulling up on one side in a gentle smirk.

Kalea frowned as she waved her hands in the water to keep afloat. "PDA?"

"Public display of affection," Hawk explained. "You know...holding hands...smiling...acting like we like each other...kissing—"

Kalea's arms stopped moving, and she sank up to her nose before she remembered she was treading water. "Kissing?" she squeaked.

"Of course." He frowned. "If we're going to make it look real, we have to do more than hold hands."

"I don't know." Kalea shook her head. "Seems like a lot to go through. How about I just call my father's bluff and send you back to the mainland? I'll be fine on my own."

Hawk shrugged. "It's your funeral. Knowing your father, he'll keep trying. Can't blame him, either. You're all he has. It would kill him to lose you." Hawk turned again to climb up the bank.

With his naked ass staring her in the face, Kalea couldn't think straight. "Fine. I'll do it."

Hawk started to turn toward her.

Kalea spun in the water. "I'll put on a show. But you and I will know it's only a show. We take it no further than what you said...PDA. In private, it's all back to a professional level. You're the bodyguard. I'm the client. Got it?" She made her demands with her back to him so she couldn't see if he was nodding.

A long pause followed her words.

Had he left?

Kalea twisted around in the water only to find Hawk

in front of her, close enough to feel his breath on her cheek.

"Don't you think we should kiss on it?" he said, a smile tugging at the corners of his lips.

"I most certainly do not," she said her voice breathy, barely more than a whisper.

"How will we make it look real if we haven't even tried a single kiss? Even stage actors have to practice kissing to get it to look natural." He took her hand and dragged her back to where she could plant her feet on the bottom of the pool and still keep her head above water.

"I'd rather practice when we're both fully clo—"

Hawk pulled her into his arms and bent until his lips hovered over hers. "No time like the present, I always say. Ready for the first act?"

"If we must," she said, her gaze on his lips, her hands flat against his chest, neither pulling him closer nor pushing him away.

"We must," he said, his warm breath feathering across her lips.

When his mouth connected with hers, she opened on a startled gasp.

He took the opportunity to sweep into hers and caress her tongue with his in a long, earth-shaking kiss, that left Kalea struggling to stand on wobbly knees.

The longer he kissed her, the weaker her resistance. Eventually, her hands slipped around his neck, drawing him closer, deepening the kiss that was never meant to be.

When her breasts pressed against his chest, an

explosion of senses set off a firestorm of lust raging through her body.

One of his hands tangled in her hair, while the other slid down to the small of her back, pulling her hips against his. The hard evidence of his desire nudged her belly.

Kalea sank into him, her pulse pounding hard in her veins, while the voice of reason was shoved firmly into the back of her head.

When at last they both needed to breathe, Hawk lifted his head and stared down at her. "I think…" he cleared his throat, "…that will be convincing."

"Now, if you'll turn your back, I'd like to get out of the water," Kalea said.

He nodded. "As you wish. Just don't take off without me."

Kalea waited until Hawk had his back to her and the shore. Then she slipped out of the water and ran for her clothes.

What had she committed to?

Being with Hawk was like dancing with dynamite. One step in the wrong direction and they'd both explode.

CHAPTER 7

HAWK TREADED WATER, waiting just long enough for Kalea to get to her clothes. He'd be damned if he stood by and let her take off without him again. He'd been hired to keep her safe. He couldn't do his job if she wasn't even close to him. Hopefully, she was good at her word and would allow them to fake a relationship. It would make it easier to keep an eye on her.

When he turned around, she had just stepped into her panties and was pulling her bra straps up over her shoulders. "You can come out of the water now," she said, and grabbed her shirt.

Hawk walked out of the pool, shoulders back, head held high. He had nothing to be embarrassed about. If she wanted to look, so be it.

Kalea turned her back on him and tugged her shirt over her wet hair and down her damp torso. With her hair pulled back in a ponytail and her T-shirt hanging down to the tops of her thighs, she looked more like a little girl than a grown woman. However, those long, curvy legs were anything but childlike.

Hawk could imagine them wrapped around his waist as he drove into her.

"Damn." He chastised himself as he tugged his jeans up his wet legs and over his buttocks. He had to stop thinking that way. Kalea was his client, not his girl-friend. Yes, they'd have to pretend otherwise, but other than showing the world they were together, in private, they had to remain professional. Bodyguard…client.

Kalea slipped into her jeans and turned to face him. "Did you say something?"

"No," he said in a short, clipped tone. Hawk jammed his feet into his boots and dragged his T-shirt over his head. "Are you ready?"

She nodded. "We should get back to the barn. I have work to do in the office. I'm heading to Oahu tomorrow for a Hawaiian Tourism Commission meeting."

"Tourism?" Hawk raised an eyebrow.

"We don't just raise cattle on the ranch. We also have a pretty big tourism branch connected to what we do here. Did you know this ranch is one of the oldest ranches in the U.S.?"

His brow furrowed. "You're kidding, right?"

"No, I'm not. My ancestors were given the acreage way back in the 1800s by a Hawaiian king for rounding up the feral cattle roaming free, destroying the native vegetation. People like coming for the Hawaiian dude ranch experience. You know, horseback riding, cattle roundups, cookouts and more. We're a significant part of the Hawaiian experience."

Hawk shook his head. "I never expected to find a ranch like this in Hawaii."

"Oh, we add a luau and traditional Hawaiian dance and stories. It wouldn't be Hawaii without them."

"Of course, it wouldn't." Hawk jammed his cowboy hat onto his head. "And do you dance for the guests?"

"Not every week, only during the annual King Kamehameha Day, when we celebrate our greatest leader who united all of the Hawaiian Islands into one kingdom. It's actually a weeklong celebration, but I only dance here at the ranch. It's our busiest week of the year."

She untied *Pupule's* reins from the bush. "Do you want to ride in the saddle?"

"No, ma'am. I'll ride behind you."

For a moment, she hesitated then shrugged. Because she was short, she held onto the side of the saddle and pulled herself up enough to stick her foot into the stirrup and then swung her leg over the horse's back.

Once she was seated, she removed her foot from the stirrup and leaned forward. "Your turn."

Relieved she wasn't going to run off without him, Hawk grabbed the saddle horn, slipped his foot into the stirrup and swung up behind Kalea, landing with a jolt on the horse's hindquarters. He slipped his foot out of the stirrup and adjusted his position.

Pupule danced in a circle with the added weight.

Hawk wrapped his arms around Kalea's waist and held on.

"Whoa, boy," she said, pulling the reins taut.

The animal came to a stop and snorted.

"Ready?" Kalea asked.

"Yes, ma'am," Hawk answered.

Kalea nudged *Pupule*'s flanks with her heels at the same time she said, "Don't call me ma'am."

The horse leaped forward, nearly unseating Hawk.

He tightened his hold on Kalea, hugging her body close to keep from sliding off.

Pupule picked his way along the trail until the trees parted, and they were once again out in the open pasture filled with tall grasses and sunshine.

As if he knew they were going home, *Pupule* picked up the pace, trotting along at a decent clip, the jarring gait rattling Hawk's teeth.

Kalea nudged the horse again, and he broke into a canter, the smoother motion easier to handle while sitting bareback.

Hawk held on, his arms around Kalea, and enjoying how close he was to her…far too much.

When they approached the gate where she'd left him earlier, she slowed their ride to a slow walk until they came close enough she could lean over and slip the latch free. "How are you doing back there?" she said, glancing over her shoulder.

"Never better," he lied. His tail bone ached, and the insides of his legs were strained from gripping the horse with his thighs. But he loved the feel and smell of good horseflesh, and the way Kalea felt in his arms. He was so close, the loose strands of her hair tickled his cheeks and nose.

Pretending an attraction to the rancher's daughter would be no problem. Keeping from falling for the woman would prove to be a major challenge. What was not to like? Kalea was tough, beautiful and could ride as well or better than he could. She liked horses and raised cattle, wore blue jeans and cowboy boots.

Add to that her exotic looks, courtesy of her Hawaiian ancestors, and she was by far the most interesting and desirable woman Hawk had ever met.

And off limits.

After they passed through the gate, Hawk leaned over to close and secure the latch. When he straightened, he smiled. "Ready?"

Kalea nodded. Before she could touch her heels to the horse's flanks, a loud blast sounded near them and a puff of dirt kicked up at *Pupule*'s hooves.

"Gunfire," Hawk said.

"Gunfire? You've got to be kidding," Kalea said.

"No, ma'am." Wrapping his arms around Kalea, Hawk gathered the reins in his hands and dug his heels into the horse's flanks.

Pupule took off like a bullet launched from a rifle. Another shot rang out, the sound barely audible over the pounding of hooves against the dirt.

A moment later, an ATV burst out of the tree line, driving parallel to the path they were on. The driver wore all black and a black helmet. He raced across the field, directly toward them.

Pupule saw the vehicle coming toward him and dodged to the side in time to miss being hit.

Hawk held tightly to Kalea with one arm around her middle, fearing he'd fly off the horse, taking her with him.

She gripped the saddle horn with both hands, keeping her seat and Hawk with her.

With no weapon with which to fight back, Hawk only had his hands and wit.

When the ATV driver circled around and came at them again, Hawk was ready.

He waited until *Pupule* dodged sideways away from the vehicle and driver. At that moment, Hawk slid off the horse's back, dropped to the ground, rolled to his feet and was up and running after the man on the ATV.

He caught up to the man as he tried to circle again and head back toward Kalea and *Pupule*.

Hawk dove through the air, grabbed the man around the shoulders and hung on, dragging the man out of his seat and onto the ground.

As soon as their attacker left the ATV, it rolled to a stop not too far from where Hawk had knocked its driver to the ground.

Before Hawk could rise, the driver scrambled to his feet and ran for the ATV.

Determined to catch him and yank off the black helmet, Hawk rolled to his feet and gave chase.

The driver made it to the ATV, leaped onto it and cranked the engine.

It roared to life and the driver hit the throttle. The back end of the vehicle spun sideways as the driver tore out.

Hawk ran toward Kalea and *Pupule*, keeping his body between the ATV and the horse and rider. If the attacker tried to get to her again, Hawk would be ready to jump him and bring him down for good.

However, the ATV headed for the woods. When the driver had gone a hundred yards, he pulled out a gun and raised it to aim.

Hawk's heart leaped into his throat. "Get down, Kalea!" He spun toward Kalea, grabbed her hand and yanked her out of the saddle as the crack of gunfire ripped through the air. Hawk caught Kalea when she hit him full in the chest. He staggered backward and fell on his ass.

As soon as he hit the ground with Kalea on top of him, he rolled her over onto her back and covered her body with his. "Stay down."

The man on the ATV fired another shot.

Anger burned through Hawk's veins. He waited for the man to fire again. When he didn't, Hawk looked up.

The ATV and rider were headed toward them again.

Hawk channeled his anger into action. "Stay down," he commanded. Then he climbed up onto his hands and knees and rushed toward the man driving the ATV, zigzagging erratically, to keep from catching a bullet.

The man fired another shot, hitting the ground in front of Hawk, then he shoved the gun into his jacket and hit the throttle, sending the four-wheeler racing toward the tree line.

Hawk would have gone after him, but he couldn't run as fast as the vehicle, and he couldn't leave Kalea alone in case there was more than one person hiding in the woods, waiting to strike. His best course of action was to get Kalea back to the ranch house surrounded by walls and people.

Hawk ran back to where he'd left Kalea lying on the

ground. It took him a moment to locate her in the field of hay.

She had risen to her knees and was peering through the tall grass when he located her. "Oh, thank goodness!" she exclaimed when she spotted him. Kalea staggered to her feet and flung herself into his arms. "I thought he'd shot you."

"I'm fine, but we need to move in case he decides to try again." Keeping her in the crook of his arm and shielding her with his own body, Hawk led her to where her horse stood with its reins hanging to the ground.

Hawk mounted, sitting in the saddle. He extended a hand to Kalea.

She took it, placed her foot on top of his boot and let him pull her up and into his lap. Her gaze locked with his. "We can't ride all the way back like this."

"We can, and we will. I'm not risking some dumbass making you his target again." Hawk reined the horse, turning it in the direction of the house and barn. He didn't waste time, but established a quick and efficient gait, sending them toward their destination. He kept a close eye on the tree line until they'd left it behind. Out in the open pasture, Hawk felt only mildly safer. The grass was so tall, it could hide other people bent on harming Kalea.

Hawk urged *Pupule* into a gallop that ate the distance between them and the ranch buildings. When they arrived at the barn, Maleko hurried out to greet them, his brow furrowed. "I was worried about you when your horse returned without its rider. I was getting ready to mount up and go looking for you two."

Kalea slid to the ground and touched the older man's arm. "We're safe, now. But someone was out there shooting at us.'

Maleko's eyes widened. "Someone shot at you?" His gaze swept over her. "Are you sure you're all right?"

Kalea nodded. "Yes. Could you please call the island police? I'd like to report what happened and send them out to look for our shooter."

"Tell them the ATV was black with a bright red flame across the gas tank. The driver wore black and had a black helmet, also with a red flame."

"I'll get right on it," Maleko said and hurried into the barn's office.

Hawk slipped off the back of the horse and stood beside Kalea. "We need to meet with your father."

Her lips thinned into a straight line. "He's going to flip."

"Yeah, but he needs to know what's going on so that he can be on the lookout for anything out of the ordinary."

She nodded. "He'll want to lock me in a padded room for the rest of my life." Kalea touched his arm. "I'm counting on you to keep that from happening. I'm hoping that as long as I have my bodyguard with me, my father won't curtail my movements overly much. I have a meeting to attend tomorrow on Oahu. I don't plan on missing it."

Hawk frowned. "I don't like the idea of you being out in the open any more than your father does." He held up his hand before she could protest. "But I understand how you don't want to be held captive. It gives your attacker too much power." While hovering close to her, he looked around the barnyard and toward the other outbuildings. "If we're going to keep you alive, you'll have to play by my rules."

Kalea stared at him for a long moment. "I'm a pretty independent kind of woman," she said.

He tipped his head. "I get that, but these are unusual circumstances. This could be a potentially lethal situation. If I'm to keep you safe, you have to do as I say."

Her lips formed a thin line for a moment, but then she sighed. "Agreed. After all, three's the charm."

Hawk frowned. "Three what? Bodyguards?"

"No," she gave him a brief smile. "Three attempts on my life. I can't expect a fourth to come out as well as the previous ones."

He sucked in a deep breath. "I only know of the first of the attacks and this one. You say there was another?"

She nodded. "My father doesn't know about it. I didn't want him to limit my mobility. Likely, you know about the man in the Phantom mask at the hardware store in Hilo...?" She waited for his response.

Hawk tipped his head. "I do."

"And this one." Kalea glance toward the pasture. "I didn't tell anyone about the man who tried to grab me in the parking lot of a small business on Main Street in Waimea."

"That's a lot closer than the initial attack in Hilo," Hawk pointed out. "You should have told your father about that one."

"He would have had the police turn Waimea upside

down and had them come out to provide twenty-four-hour protection."

"And that's a bad idea?" Hawk asked, his eyebrows rising.

"He would have forbidden my riding out on the ranch. I felt it was the safest place since the other attacks had happened in a town and a city." She sighed. "After today, I guess I was wrong in my assumption."

"I think so," he said between clenched jaws.

"And my father and I were wrong assuming my attacker only wanted to kidnap me for ransom. Apparently, whoever is after me wants me dead." She pressed a hand to her mouth, her eyes wide. "Why? What have I done?"

"I don't know. But I think you're going to be stuck with me until we figure this out and catch whoever is after you."

Maleko hurried out of the barn. "The police are on their way. They'll be here in less than fifteen minutes." He took the reins from Hawk. "I'll take care of *Pupule*. You need to go inside and tell your father what's happening before the authorities arrive." He took *Pupule* into the barn to remove his saddle and brush him down.

"My father's going to freak," Kalea whispered, her lips pressing into a tight line.

Hawk placed a hand at the small of her back. "We have a plan. Let's go with it."

"I need to be at that meeting tomorrow in Honolulu. He's going to put his foot down and say I can't go."

"I'll be with you, wherever you go. That's why he

hired me." He gave her a gentle nudge toward the house. "Come on, we'll face him together."

"You don't understand," Kalea said. "Since my mother died, my father has been a worried hen, hovering over everything I do."

"Then it's up to us to convince him you'll be all right," Hawk tried to reassure her. Not that he was that much more confident than she was. After the shooter had fired on them, Hawk wasn't sure about much. Thankfully, the man had missed. A good sniper wouldn't have made that mistake.

They entered the house and went straight to Mr. Parkman's study. The door was open, and the ranch owner was seated with his back to the room, his gaze on the computer monitor in front of him.

Hawk knocked his knuckles against the doorframe.

Parkman turned immediately, a smile stretching across his face. "Hawk, Kalea, please, come in."

Hawk ushered Kalea across the threshold and closed the door behind them.

As they progressed across the floor, the older man must have seen something in their expressions. "What's wrong?"

"Now, Daddy, don't get upset…" Kalea started.

"Starting a sentence like that is a surefire way to get a man upset." Parkman frowned. "What's wrong?"

Hawk touched Kalea's arm. "Let me."

She nodded and took a seat on the sofa near her father's desk.

Hawk remained standing as he gave the older man the situation report.

As Hawk spoke, Mr. Parkman's frown deepened. "Dear Lord," he finally said, his face pale as he pinched the bridge of his nose. "I thought kidnapping was the motivation. I'd give all my money to anyone who took my daughter from me. But this…" He waved a hand in the air. "You can't buy back a life." His gaze went to his daughter. "Oh, baby, I'm so sorry. If I'd known he wanted to kill you, I wouldn't have let you outside the house until we figured out who was behind the attacks."

Kalea's gaze went to Hawk. "I told you he'd flip."

Hawk nodded at Kalea. "And rightly so. His only daughter is the target of a psycho-killer. I'd be upset, too." He turned to Mr. Parkman. "You hired me to protect your daughter. I'm still here. I'm still committed to the task."

Parkman shot a glance between him and Kalea.

"She knows," Hawk said with a smile. "And we'd come to an agreement, even before the shooting began. Your daughter has agreed to let me protect her. But to do so without alerting her attacker to the fact I'm a bodyguard, we've decided we should stay very close together at all times. Since Kalea has never been that close to a hired hand, we think it's best we pretend I'm her boyfriend. That way, it's more natural if I'm around her all the time. Right now, the three of us are the only ones who know why I'm really here."

Her father remained silent for a moment, his gaze going from his daughter to Hawk. At last, his shoulders slumped. "How will she say you two met?"

Kalea smiled. "We met when I was in college in San Diego. I had a friend whose brother was at the Navy

SEAL BUD/S training when I was going to school. He could have introduced us."

Parkman nodded. "It fits. Why is he here now and not sooner? And why did he come to us as a *paniolo*?"

"We reconnected on social media, and he hired on to prove himself to you and me."

"Okay, as long as we all have the story straight." Parkman looked from Kalea to Hawk. "I still want to confine you to the house until we find the shooter."

Kalea shook her head. "I can't hide. We don't know how long it will take to find the man. In the meantime, I have work to do. Not everything about this ranch can be passed off to someone else to accomplish."

Hawk admired her confidence and determination.

And she was so sexy with her shoulders thrown back and her brown eyes flashing. Her hair had dried on the ride back from the pool, curling down her back in tight, dark waves.

Hawk had the urge to run his fingers through her hair and bury his face in the tresses. She was beautiful and passionate about her work with the ranch. If she was even half as passionate in bed…

He yanked his thoughts back to the present and the woman's father in front of him, heat rising up his neck into his cheeks. "Sir, I'll protect her wherever she needs to go."

"If someone is shooting at her, you can't anticipate from which direction the bullets will come." Parkman shook his head. "One person can't possibly protect her from all angles."

Kalea's chin lifted. "I won't be confined to the house.

I have a meeting tomorrow in Honolulu that I've had on the schedule for a few months. I can't miss it."

"I'll go in your place," her father offered.

"No, Dad, you need to stick to the ranching. I've been working with the buyers one-on-one. They're used to me and my methods. I don't want to change things on them now. We're close to making one of the biggest deals in Parkman Ranch history. I can't let it fall apart because some sociopath is gunning for me."

Her father winced, as did Hawk.

Hawk stepped forward. "Sir, I'll be with her and make sure she has sufficient coverage to keep her out of harm's way."

"How do you intend to get there?" Parkman asked. "Flying commercial puts you in front of a lot of people you don't know."

"Then I'll go in the ranch plane."

Hawk shot a glance toward Kalea. The ranch had a plane?

Her father rubbed his chin, his eyes narrowing. "It would keep you from crowded places."

"Exactly. And I'd fly into Honolulu into the general aviation side of the airport." She leaned forward where she was seated on the sofa. "Just getting away from the Big Island might get me out of the line of fire. All of the attacks have been here."

Her father nodded. "Perhaps you should stay over on Oahu until we sort this out."

Kalea frowned. "I wouldn't go that far, but the break will give the police a day to investigate and maybe find who's bothering me."

Her father snorted. "'Bothering' sounds so mild. Someone *shooting* at you is more than a bother."

She smiled. "True. So, I'm on for Oahu tomorrow, as planned?"

Her father's eyes narrowed to slits.

Hawk waited for the final verdict.

"You're on," Mr. Parkman said. "But the first sign of danger, and I want you back here where I can keep an eye on you."

Kalea jumped up and gave her father a kiss on the cheek. "Thank you, Daddy." She turned to Hawk. "We're flying to Oahu tomorrow. You might want to pack an overnight bag in case we have to stay a night."

Hawk nodded. The thought of being alone with Kalea overnight made his groin tighten. They'd have to have adjoining rooms with a connecting door left open. He wouldn't leave her alone in a hotel room any other way.

Alone with Kalea in a hotel room could be as dangerous to Hawk as being alone with her in a secluded pool. No matter what, he couldn't lose focus. Kalea's life depended on his remaining combat ready.

CHAPTER 8

AFTER THE HAWAII Police came and took her statement, Kalea left her father's study and ran up the stairs to shower and change for dinner. The thought of flying to Oahu with Hawk had her heart thumping against her ribs. It would be an overnight trip if the meeting lasted late into the day.

She grabbed a dress, panties and a clean bra and hurried across the hall to the bathroom. As she did, she glanced toward the staircase.

Hawk reached the landing, paused and looked her way.

Her pulse quickened, and heat rose up her neck into her cheeks. All she could think about was how they'd kissed as they'd stood naked in the pool such a short time ago. Her body burned with her core at the center of the fire.

As if frozen in time, neither one of them moved.

A door closing downstairs broke through Kalea's consciousness. Hugging her clothes to her chest, she dove into the bathroom, closed the door behind her and leaned against it. Her breathing came in ragged breaths as though she'd been running.

Why did the man have that effect on her? He was only a man her father had paid to protect her. She'd just met him less than twenty-four hours before, and she meant nothing to him.

But that kiss…

Kalea turned on the water in the shower, set it to lukewarm and stripped out of her clothes. A moment later she stepped beneath the tepid spray, praying it would cool her fevered flesh and bring her back to reality. She couldn't start anything with Hawk. He was a temporary fixture in her day-to-day life. Once the threat to her was resolved, he'd be on his way back to the mainland. Kalea would remain where she belonged, continuing to support and eventually be responsible for the family legacy of Parkman Ranch. Over three hundred employees depended on the continuation of her heritage.

As the water sluiced over her shoulders and down her torso, she wondered what it would be like to leave Hawaii, to dare to live somewhere else for the rest of her life. Like the wilds of Montana, where the snow got so deep they had to shovel their way out of their houses. Where there were bears, elk and antelope, running wild and free. What would it be like to snuggle up to a fireplace on a cold winter's night with the man you loved?

She leaned her head back and let the water run over her head and eyes. Who was she kidding? Other than short vacations to other places in the world, Kalea's life was tied to the Big Island of Hawaii. Her roots ran as deep as the base of Mauna Kea, almost twenty thousand feet beneath the surface of the ocean. Hawaii was her home, her culture and her life. Living elsewhere wasn't an option. Not that anyone was asking. But if he did, she was destined to say no. What was the point of falling for someone who clearly didn't want to stay?

Though her mind told her a relationship with her bodyguard was fruitless, her body continued to react to the mere fact he was under the same roof and physically close. If he chose to, he could knock on the door. She could let him in, and they could share the shower, picking up where they'd left off in the pool.

Kalea closed her eyes and imagined running soapy hands over his body and down his long, thickly muscled legs. Her breath caught, and her heart skipped several beats before pounding away again. She turned to let the spray pelt her face, reaching for the handle to make the water even cooler until she shivered, and finally, switched off the shower and got out.

She wasn't as cool and collected as she would have preferred, but the cold water had helped to bring her closer to her normal level of self-control.

After toweling her skin and hair dry, she dressed quickly, flung open the door and nearly walked into the rock-solid wall of Hawk's muscular chest.

"Oh." Kalea raised a hand to rest against his T-shirt. "I didn't expect you to be standing there."

"I was about to knock to see how much longer you would be." He smiled. "You look lovely."

Kalea glanced down at the pale seafoam green,

Hawaiian-print dress she'd chosen to wear for dinner. She hadn't brought shoes into the bathroom with her, so she stood in her bare feet, feeling small and somewhat vulnerable in front of Hawk's tall frame.

He lifted his hand and gripped her elbow. "Kalea, about today..."

Her fingers curled into his shirt. God, she hoped he wouldn't say their kiss had been a mistake.

"What happened in the pool..." He shook his head.

Before he could continue, she pressed her palm flat to his chest. "Don't worry. I don't expect any promises or announcements of undying devotion. What happened could have happened to anyone in the same circumstances. Let's just forget it." She forced a smile to her face and kept her real feelings locked down. There was no way in hell she'd forget that kiss. And it hadn't happened to just anyone. It had happened to her...with Hawk.

His grip tightened on her elbow. "What I was going to say was that I shouldn't have taken advantage of you." His gaze bore down into hers. "But I have no regrets. I wouldn't have kissed you if I hadn't wanted to." Hawk gave her a crooked smile. "And I wanted to."

Her breath catching in her throat, Kalea's knees wobbled. "You did?"

"Yes. But I'll do my best to be more professional from here on out. I can't go around kissing my client. I'm sure there's something in the bodyguard's rule book that states you aren't supposed to kiss the person you're guarding."

She stared up into his green eyes. "I didn't take you for much of a rule-follower."

He dipped his head lower until his mouth was close to hers. "Can't say that I am." He brushed his lips across hers. "Damn. There I go again, breaking all the rules." Then he drew her into his arms and kissed her longer, harder and deeper than she could ever have imagined, leaving her breathless and weak-kneed.

When he finally set her at arm's length, he shook his head. "This could be bad."

Kalea touched her fingertips to her lips. "Why?"

"I need to maintain focus, but all I can focus on is your lips and how much I want to keep kissing them." He drew in a deep breath and squared his shoulders. "I might have to fire myself from this job. If I were smart, I'd call my boss. You need someone who isn't going to lose his mind every time you're near." He stepped away from her, moving to the side to allow her to cross the hallway into her bedroom. "You should probably go before I forget who we are again."

She started that direction and stopped. He was right. To do his job, he couldn't be distracted. If he thought he couldn't get the focus he needed, he'd get someone else to do the job and leave. Though Kalea had never wanted the constraints of having someone follow her around twenty-four-seven, she couldn't imagine anyone else but Hawk in that role.

She squared her shoulders and turned to him, taking a page from his original playbook and donning a poker face. "I don't want a different bodyguard. You said we had to pretend we were an actual couple. I was just doing my part. It was all an act. You don't have to worry that I'm attracted to you. I'll have no problem keeping it professional, unless we need to…act." She stared at him, holding that straight face, refusing to let any of her internal warring emotions show through.

His eyes narrowed for a brief moment, and then he nodded. "Good. Let's keep it that way. But if I slip at all, I'm calling Hank and asking him to send a replacement. Keeping you alive is the end goal here."

"As it should be." Kalea turned and entered her room, closing the door behind her before she relaxed her face and let the tears slip down her cheeks. She brushed them away. Life had gotten way too complicated. She wanted a man who wanted her, but if he had her, he'd have to leave. She couldn't step out of her house without being fully aware of the target she presented to any crackpot sniper who decided she needed to be wiped off the face of the earth. And tomorrow, she'd fly to Oahu with the man who made her heart flutter and her knees turn to Jell-O. But she'd have to pretend they were a couple while pretending she didn't care about him. How messed up was that?

How she wished she could talk to her mother at times like these. She would have had the kind of advice Kalea needed in the ways of the heart and dealing with men. Her mother had captured the heart of the great John Parkman and held it in her hand until the day she'd died and beyond. Kalea's father had yet to get over her mother's death, even though it had been years. She wondered if he'd ever marry again.

When Clarise had come to work for Parkman

Ranch, Kalea thought she might be the one to break her father's long reign of grief. He'd shown more interest in her than any other woman he'd come into contact with since his wife's death. But he still hadn't committed to a relationship, much less a first date with the woman.

Clarise wasn't much older than Kalea, but if her father fell in love again, she wouldn't stand in the way, no matter how old or young his chosen partner was. She wanted her father to be happy.

Would she ever feel comfortable confiding in her father's new bride like the mother she'd lost…? No. Kalea was old enough to figure out her own problems. But she still missed her mother and wished she could talk to her.

Kalea's mother would have loved Hawk. Of that, she was certain. He was handsome, strong, protective and sincere. If only he wasn't an employee, things might have worked out differently. But he was, and they couldn't.

Kalea entered her room and pulled on strappy sandals to go with the Hawaiian-print dress. Smoothing a brush through her wavy hair, she pulled it straight back from her forehead. She debated putting on makeup but decided against it. She shouldn't encourage Hawk by making more of an effort to look nice. She wasn't going to seduce him, and he wasn't going to take her up on a seduction, even if she tried.

Purely professional. That's how it will be from now on, she told herself.

Armed with that thought, she left her room and descended the staircase to the ground floor to find

Clarise in the foyer with a man she'd seen before, dressed in a gray suit and a red tie.

Clarise smiled as she approached. "Kalea, you remember Tyler Beckett, the CEO of Prestige Spa Resort on Maui, don't you?"

Beckett extended a hand. "Miss Parkman, it's nice to see you again."

She shook the man's hand, her grip stronger than his weak one. "Aren't you the man who's been trying to convince my father to build a resort on Parkman Ranch?"

Beckett nodded. "Yes, ma'am. I don't give up easily. Especially when I see a lot of potential in a particular project."

"My father isn't interested in building a resort on Parkman Ranch." She faced Clarise with a forced smile. "I thought he told you that in no uncertain terms."

Clarise's smooth, elegant brow wrinkled slightly. "It's been a while since he's spoken with Tyler. Perhaps he will listen this time."

Kalea could already tell dinner would be strained. Her father had never wanted to deal with the tourism side of Parkman Ranch. Though he was an astute businessman, he was a cattle rancher, not a people pleaser. He preferred working with the animals. Like Hawk.

The only reason there was a tourism aspect to the ranch was because his grandmother had insisted it was their duty to share the history of the ranch with those interested, and to show people from the mainland the amazing things they were doing as the largest cattle ranch on the islands. He'd continued to support his grandmother's dream but had put his foot down on the subject of expanding beyond the few hundred people who made Parkman Ranch their vacation destination each year.

"Ah, Clarise, I didn't think you'd be here for dinner this evening since you came last night." Kalea's father emerged from his study with a smile on his face. That smile turned downward when he spotted Tyler Beckett. "Beckett, this is a surprise." He held out his hand, though his gaze went to Clarise, his eyes narrowing. "Did I miss the memo?" He shook Beckett's hand and released it quickly.

Clarise turned on her hundred-watt charm with a brilliant smile. She leaned up on her toes and pressed a kiss to Kalea's father's cheek. "I didn't think you'd mind. It's always good to hear the news from the other islands and see what's trending. I called ahead to let the chef know I was coming with one guest."

Kalea swallowed a snort. Clarise was in charge of marketing everything to do with Parkman Ranch, from advertising the excellent beef they raised to ensuring the dude ranch got the proper notice in the Hawaiian travel brochures each year. She made no secret that she wanted to expand tourism on the Big Island. Oahu was the main hub of Hawaiian tourism, with Maui second. Though the Big Island was the largest in land mass, it was third in annual number of visiting tourists. Clarise wanted to increase the number of visitors to the island by giving them more options at the Parkman Ranch.

Her father wasn't interested. He liked Clarise, her beauty, wit and determination, but she wasn't winning any popularity contest with John Parkman with the direction she wished to take the ranch.

Kalea didn't worry. Her father could handle his marketing manager.

Clarise clapped her hands together. "Are we ready to be seated?" she said, as if she were the hostess, not the guest.

"Just waiting on one more," her father said.

"Sorry to keep you waiting," a deep voice said from behind Kalea. Hawk joined them, slipped an arm around Kalea's waist and dropped a kiss on the top of her head. He held out a hand to Beckett. "Jace Hawkins."

Heat spread throughout Kalea's body from where Hawk's hand rested. Pretending to be a couple while keeping a professional distance would be impossible.

"Tyler Beckett." The resort CEO shook Hawk's hand and raised an eyebrow toward Clarise.

"Mr. Hawkins is the new *paniolo* on the ranch." Her brow furrowed, and she raised her own brow at Hawk's familiarity with Kalea. "Am I missing something?"

"Actually, we didn't want to make a big deal of it, but Kalea and I go back to when she went to college in San Diego. I wasn't completely up front with Mr. Parkman when I interviewed for the *paniolo* position. I knew Kalea, but I wanted to get the job based on my own merit, not because I'm in love with his daughter."

Clarise's forehead pinched. "In love?" She looked to Kalea's father. "Did you know any of this?"

Her father shook his head and grinned. "Nope. Not until they returned from horseback riding. Then it all came out. I couldn't be happier for my little girl. About time she found someone to love." He winked at her. "And Hawk seems to be a good guy, with Kalea's best interests and happiness at heart." He clapped a hand to Hawk's shoulder. "I'd be happy to have him as part of the family."

"Whoa, Daddy." Kalea laughed. "Don't rush things. One, we just reconnected and are getting acquainted again. And two, he hasn't asked or put a ring on my finger yet." She forced a smile up at Hawk. "I don't want you to scare him off."

"Right, right." Her father squeezed Hawk's shoulder. "There's plenty of time to figure out I'm a pushy father...*after* the wedding." Again, he winked. "Come on, let's eat. These two have had a demanding day, they need food to replenish their reserves." He walked on one side of Hawk, while Kalea walked on the other, leading the other two guests into the formal dining room.

Ule had the table set with fine china, polished silverware and crystal goblets.

"What's the special occasion?" Kalea's father asked when Ule entered carrying a roasted chicken surrounded by asparagus and cooked carrots.

"Miss Sanders asked for the china." Ule set the platter on the table.

"I hope you don't mind," Clarise hurried to say. "Such beautiful things should be used, not hidden away in a cabinet."

Kalea's father stared at the china, his gaze farther away than the table.

The last time they'd used the china had been years

ago, before her mother had died. They'd gotten it out to celebrate her last birthday on earth.

Kalea placed a hand on her father's shoulder. "The table is gorgeous. Mother would have loved that the china you gave her is being used."

He nodded and covered her hand on his shoulder. "You're right." He pulled out the chair beside his for Kalea.

She slipped into the seat and waited as the others took seats around the table.

Ule returned with another platter of *manapau,* the puffy buns filled with chicken or beans Kalea loved so much.

"Thank you, Ule," Kalea said and smiled. Her mother had made the Hawaiian treat at every holiday. She wondered what point Ule was trying to make by serving *manapau.* Perhaps he'd made the traditional dish to honor her memory. Whatever the chef's reason, Kalea appreciated the gesture and selected one from the plate.

Hawk sat beside Kalea. Clarise and Beckett took the seats on the opposite side of the table.

Kalea's father carved the roasted chicken and served a portion of the meat and vegetables to Kalea, Hawk and himself before passing the platter and serving fork to Clarise.

Conversation at the dinner table revolved around the price of beef and how different advertising had helped disseminate news about the beef available in local markets on the islands. Clarise had contracted a local communications company to produce a television commercial. The ad on television had generated interest from supermarkets that had been getting their beef shipped in from the mainland. So many people on the mainland, as well as in Hawaii itself, were unaware of the amount of beef raised on the Big Island. The ad campaigns were part of an effort to educate the people of Hawaii on what their state had to offer.

"The ads appear to be working," Clarise said. "Over the past month, sales have increased, and we've had a number of inquiries asking for pricing and delivery dates."

"That's excellent," John said, "considering those ads cost a fortune."

"It takes money to make money," Clarise reminded him. "And I'm keeping track of the return on investment. If we make a few more sales than normal, we'll have earned back all that money and more."

"That's why I pay you the big bucks," Kalea's father said.

"I'm sure what you pay in advertising for your ranch operations is a mere fraction of what we have to pay in the resort business," Beckett said. "We're in competition with so many other resorts, we have to pour significant amounts of money into our advertising budgets to be seen in the Hawaiian tourism trade."

"All the more reason to stick to what we do best," John Parkman said. "Raising cattle is what we do. Catering to tourists is just a side operation."

"Oh, but it could be so much more." Beckett leaned forward. "Advertising isn't a four-letter word. It's a necessary part of the resort and tourism industry." He nodded toward Kalea. "Even your little attempt at inviting guests to stay on the ranch wouldn't get noticed if you weren't included in some kind of advertising, isn't that right, Miss Parkman?" He raised an eyebrow. "Aren't you attending the Hawaiian Tourism Commission meeting tomorrow in Honolulu?"

She nodded. "I am."

"And if you didn't attend, Parkman Ranch wouldn't be listed in the tourism guide they produce, would it?" Beckett waited for her response.

Kalea shrugged. "They only support those who make the effort to show up."

"And Parkman Ranch has the added advantage of being part of Hawaiian heritage. It's been in existence since the early 1800s," Beckett stated, though the Parkmans were completely aware of the facts. "Can you imagine how many more people you could reach if you put money into advertising your guest facilities?"

"We maintain one hundred percent occupancy," Kalea said. "Most of that is word-of-mouth. We only care about the Tourism brochure because it lists heritage sites."

"I bet if you had an upscale resort on the ranch, you'd fill it as well," Beckett said. "Easily."

"That's just the point." Color rose in John Parkman cheeks. "We don't want more people. The number of guests we already get is more than enough. I don't want the headache of entertaining more. And I don't want them interfering with our primary purpose, which is raising cattle."

Kalea didn't like it when her father got upset. And he was well on his way to upset.

"But—" Beckett started.

Clarise touched a hand briefly to Beckett's arm. "Ule is such a good cook. This chicken practically melts in my mouth. John, what will you do when Ule retires? Has he started training another chef to fill his shoes when he's ready to leave?"

"Ule assures me he's going to stay until he can't cook anymore," Kalea said. "He figures he's got another twenty or so years left in him." She didn't want Ule going anywhere. He was part of her family.

"For that matter," Clarise continued, "have you considered what will happen when there are no more Parkmans to run the ranch?"

"I haven't given up hope of Kalea giving me grand-children," he smiled across at Kalea.

"Dad." Kalea frowned briefly but patted her father's hand.

"I know, I know. Stop trying to run your life." Her father sighed. "It's really too bad arranged marriages have gone out of style. I'd already have half a dozen grandkids running wild around the place, if I had my way."

"Dad…" Kalea repeated.

"Okay, I'll lay off." He squeezed her hand. "I only want you to be happy. If having half a dozen kids makes you happy, even better." He winked. "No pressure."

Her cheeks flushed with heat, Kalea stared down at her food, no longer hungry. She planned on having chil-dren, but just hadn't met the right man. As she neared thirty, she'd worried she never would. What man wanted a woman who could ride horses and herd cattle? Most of them wanted a woman who could cook, clean and raise children as well as hold down an office job.

Kalea wanted a man who wanted her for herself. A man who wanted a partner. One who would share in all responsibilities of running a house, bringing in money and raising children. She liked working hard and wanted someone who would appreciate and respect her for that, not take it away.

She shot a sideways glance at Hawk.

He reached beneath the table, found her hand on her lap, and gave it a gentle squeeze.

Her heart warmed and swelled. She wished she could find a man like Hawk. He could ride almost as well as she could. He knew horses and cattle and worked hard for what he wanted, as evidenced by his success as a Navy SEAL.

"Mr. Parkman, Clarise makes a good point. Have you thought about what would happen to Parkman Ranch if there were no more Parkmans to pass it on to?" Beckett asked.

"I've been working with an attorney. The ranch and all its assets have been rolled into a trust. Should something happen to either me or Kalea, the trust would be run by a trustee. The operations would continue on as usual. All the employees would still have their jobs."

"Where would the profits go?" Clarise asked.

"I've identified a few charities that would benefit from them, as well as some scholarships for indigenous

Hawaiians who need a hand with college or trade school tuition."

Kalea's father finished his meal and sat back. "Why don't we take coffee out on the porch. It's a beautiful night. It would be a shame to waste it indoors."

Kalea helped Ule clear the table while the others headed out onto the porch.

She was washing plates in the sink when Hawk entered, carrying more dishes.

"You don't have to help," she said. "Ule doesn't usually like anyone else in his kitchen, but I don't like leaving him with all the work."

"I don't mind help in the kitchen." Ule reached around her for a washcloth. "I just don't like it when whoever helps doesn't know where I keep everything."

Kalea chuckled. "That's why he doesn't mind me helping. I know where he hides things."

Ule harrumphed. "She put my potato peeler in the drawer with the spatulas."

"Once," Kalea added. "I know not to do that now." She shook her head. "He's impossible."

"You're impossible," Ule shot back. "Little *Ali'i*."

"I'm not a princess," Kalea said.

Ule left the kitchen to return to the dining room, washcloth in hand.

"I'll dry, if you can find me a towel," Hawk offered.

She fished one out of a drawer and handed it to him, thinking, *just like this*. Partners in all tasks, from washing dishes to castrating steers.

"What did you say?" Hawk took a china plate from her hands.

A rush of embarrassment filled her cheeks with warmth. "Did I say something?" Had she spoken out loud?

"Yeah, something about partners in castrating steers." He chuckled. "Did I hear that right?"

Kalea mentally kicked herself. God, she had to be better at hiding her emotions and keeping her comments about the perfect partner to herself. She cast a glance at the man who was quickly ticking off the long list of criteria that had kept her from finding that man of her dreams.

CHAPTER 9

Kalea handed Hawk the last plate to dry, reached around him and lifted the stack of dry plates. "I must be daydreaming. Wanna go for a walk when we're done?"

Still curious about her comment involving castrating steers, Hawk thought it better to let the subject drop. "Sure it's safe to wander around outside?" He dried the plate, laid it on the stack, and then took them from her. "Lead the way."

Kalea led him back into the dining room where the china cabinet stood at one end. "My mother ordered this china for their five-year anniversary. She wanted fine dinnerware for when they entertained guests." She chuckled softly. "They didn't often have guests. My father prefers to have dinner with just his family."

"How often does he invite Miss Sanders to have dinner with you two?"

Kalea frowned. "I'm not exactly sure he invites her. I think she invites herself. Perhaps I need to have a talk with her."

"I'm sure your father can handle his employee."

Kalea opened the cabinet and held the door while Hawk placed the plates in the stack where they belonged. "Yeah, but he shouldn't have to *handle* her." She closed the cabinet.

"Your father seems like a man who would tell someone how he feels if he felt strongly enough about it."

"You're right." Kalea nodded. "Shall we go out and prove to Clarise and Mr. Beckett that we're more than just strangers faking a relationship?"

He nodded, held out his arm and waited for her to slip her hand around his elbow. When she did, he realized how much he liked it there and had to remind himself this was all just for show.

They left the house through the back door that led onto the porch.

Mr. Parkman, Clarise and Mr. Beckett were seated, looking out over the pasture with several horses grazing contentedly on fresh green grass.

Clarise had chosen to sit on the porch swing beside Mr. Parkman, while Beckett sat in a seat nearby.

"Going for a walk?" Parkman asked.

Kalea nodded. "It's a lovely evening."

"Don't forget Lani will be here in thirty minutes for your hula lesson."

Kalea's body sagged. "Right. I'll be back in time for it." She tightened her hold on Hawk's arm and hurried him down the steps and out toward the barn. Once they were beyond earshot, she shook her head. "Hula lessons. If I hadn't promised my mother I'd continue the tradition, I'd have given up on the dance a long time ago."

"Hula?" Hawk laughed softly. "I can't picture you dancing in front of anyone."

She stopped short, bringing him to a stop with her. "Why?"

Realizing his mistake, he backpaddled. "Not that I think you'd be bad at it, but it seems odd for someone who's an expert horsewoman and prefers to be out riding over anything else."

She drew in a deep breath and let it out. "I do prefer riding to dancing. It's just that I've done the same dance year after year for the annual King Kamehameha celebration. I know it by heart. I shouldn't have to practice it every year."

He couldn't hold back a smile. "This, I have to see."

"If you're still around, I'll give you front row tickets so you can laugh at little Kalea trying to dance the hula." Her lips twisted into a smirk. "You'll get a good chuckle. And the costumes are so…"

"Sexy?"

"Not jeans," she ended on a flat note. "But hopefully, you won't have to endure the celebration. By then, I hope they will have captured the attacker and put him away. You won't have any reason to stay in Hawaii after that. You can go back to your precious Montana where it snows six months out of the year."

"Seven," he corrected. "In fact, I've known it to snow in July."

"There you go. We don't get snow that often, unless you count Mauna Kea." She nodded toward the mountain peak, rising toward the heavens in the distance. The sun was slipping into the horizon, making the mountain a dark silhouette in the evening sky.

"It's pretty impressive. I remember the first time I saw its snowcapped peaks when we were flying over the island on our way to practice extractions." He remembered staring at the mountain through the open door of the Osprey helicopter. It had reminded him so much of his home in Montana, he'd had a sudden bout of homesickness. Thankfully, the training took his mind off home and brought him back to the task at hand.

Funny, the mountain didn't make him homesick this time. After riding horses with Kalea that day, he'd felt more at home there in Hawaii than he'd ever thought he could. Definitely more so than when he'd been stationed on Oahu among the palm trees and city lights.

"Montana is your home?" she asked.

"Yes, it is."

"When I was in school in San Diego, all I could think about was finishing quickly so that I could get back home to the ranch. I was so homesick, I finished college in three years."

"I get that."

"Was it that way for you?"

"I spent fifteen years on active duty, thirteen as a SEAL. I looked forward to my visits home, but it wasn't until last year that I knew I had to get out or lose who I was. I needed the wide-open spaces and something besides sand and dust in my eyes. I think I deployed once too often. I saw too many of the people I cared for die."

She leaned against his arm. "I'm sorry."

He shrugged. "It's that part of the job description, they don't advertise well." He came to a halt by the fence where they'd stood the night before. He scanned the surroundings, growing shadowy as the sun sank below the horizon.

"I bet you were looking forward to going back to Montana," she said softly.

"I admit, I was surprised when Hank sent me here instead of Montana."

"Surprised and disappointed?" she quizzed, looking up at him, her dark eyes liquid pools of ink in her face.

"At first."

"And now?"

He shook his head. "I never expected a place like this ranch could exist here in Hawaii. It reminds me of the ranch I grew up on. It has all the requisite animals."

"Horses and cattle," she filled in.

"What about you?" He turned to her. "You wanted to get back home after school. Have you ever thought of living anywhere else?"

She shook her head. "I want to visit other places. I'd love to travel. But I always want to return to where I belong. Hawaii is my heritage. My mother's people have been here farther back than written records. My father's people made this their home over two hundred years ago." She smiled. "I can't imagine living anywhere else. I might complain about dancing for the King Kamehameha celebration, but I really look forward to honoring the king that united the islands into one kingdom. I love the traditions and the stories we tell through dance. It's part of my family, my heritage…me."

He turned her to face him. "You're an amazing woman. Sometimes, I don't know if you're the rough and tumble cowgirl or the Hawaiian native filled with the charm of your people." Hawk tipped her chin up to the lingering light, fading to black as night crept over the land. "I think you're both, all wrapped in one beautiful package. And here I go again, about to break the rules. Please tell me to stop, and I will. Otherwise, I'm going to kiss you."

"Don't," she said, placing her hand on his chest.

He hesitated, his lips so close to hers, he could feel the warmth of her breath.

Her fingers curled into his shirt, bringing his body closer. "Don't stop. You need to take one for the team. I think they're watching." Then she leaned up on her toes and pressed her lips to his.

He gathered her into his arms and held her close, returning the pressure on her mouth until her lips parted. Then all restraint failed him, and he dove in, caressing her tongue with his in a gentle glide. For a long moment, they stood melded together in the darkening gloom.

When at last, Hawk lifted his head, he leaned his forehead against hers. "That ought to convince anyone watching."

"It convinced me," she said, her voice airy, as if she couldn't quite catch her breath.

"We should call it a night." He smoothed her hair

back behind her ears. "I know I'll be sore from riding today."

She nodded. "You'll be sore for a couple of days. That's why it's important to get back as soon as possible so we can ride again. The more you ride, the sooner your muscles relearn. We'll leave after breakfast tomorrow. I want to get to Oahu before noon."

"Yes, ma'am." He held out his arm again.

"For appearances sake, you should call me Kalea," she said.

"Kalea," he said, his tongue rolling over her name like he was trying it on for the fit. "It suits you."

They walked back to the house, arm-in-arm. When they climbed the porch, they found Kalea's father standing in front of Clarise and Beckett, who were just rising to their feet.

"Are you leaving?" Kalea asked.

Clarise nodded. "Tyler is driving back to Hilo tonight, and he's dropping me off in Waimea before he heads out." She turned to Mr. Parkman. "John, will I see you tomorrow for lunch?" She touched his arm with more familiarity than an employee to her boss.

Hawk looked toward Kalea.

Her brow wrinkled for a moment, but then smoothed.

Was she jealous of Clarise's casual flirtation with her father?

If she was, did it matter?

Would she feel the same about staying in Hawaii if her father remarried and she moved down in importance in John Parkman's life?

A father remarrying had a way of upending the lives of his children from his previous marriage, even if they were grown. If John Parkman remarried, his assets not attached to his trust would go to his wife, if he hadn't specified in a will that they were to go elsewhere.

Hawk would hate to see Kalea shifted to second place by a potential stepmother. Especially if that stepmother was closer to her age than to her father's.

After the pair departed, Mr. Parkman entered the house and moved toward his study. "I have work to do. Please excuse me."

"Daddy, you work too hard. You need to take it easier, or you'll give yourself a heart attack." Kalea grabbed his arm and turned him toward a sitting room. "Come, sit with us and relax."

"I suppose I could," he said, allowing his daughter to steer him into the sitting room with a couple of sofas and a lounge chair all in shades of gray and white.

No sooner had they entered the room than a phone rang on a table by the door.

Parkman lifted the phone out of its cradle. "Parkman Ranch, John speaking."

Hawk didn't like to eavesdrop, but they were all in the same room. Short of walking out, he couldn't help but hear one side of the conversation.

John's grip on the phone grew tighter. "You found the ATV? Where? Do you know who it belongs to? Nathaniel Bowman. I know him. He's been in and out of trouble all his life. I'm surprised he's even out of jail. Last I heard, he was serving time for assault and battery when he robbed a convenience store in Hilo. What's he doing back here?"

Parkman's face paled. "Damn." He pinched the bridge of his nose. "How?" The ranch owner appeared to have aged in the few short minutes he'd been on the phone. "Thank you for letting me know. Please keep me informed about the investigation." When he finally ended the call, he looked toward Kalea. "Nate Bowman was the guy on the ATV who attacked you this afternoon."

Kalea stepped forward and laid her hand on her father's arm. "That's good they found him."

Her father shook his head. "They found him dead."

"Dead?" Kalea's brow furrowed.

Nodding, her father pulled her into his arms and hugged her tight. "He was murdered," he whispered.

Kalea hugged him back. For a long moment, they held each other.

Hawk felt superfluous in the family moment but couldn't leave. His job was to keep Kalea safe. After a long moment, Hawk asked, "Did they say how he was murdered."

John Parkman looked up, his eyes haunted, the lines in his face deeper than before. "Shot in the chest. Point blank."

"Wow." Kalea stepped out of her father's embrace and paced across the room and back. "Do they have any idea who might have done it?"

Her father shook his head. "None."

"Did they find the bullet?"

"They did. And they sent it to the state crime lab to identify the type weapon." Kalea's father's hands tightened into fists. "I don't think you should go to Oahu tomorrow."

Kalea shook her head. "Just because someone shot Nate, doesn't mean they're going to get to me. We don't even know why Nate was after me in the first place. What if whoever killed him was trying to protect me?"

Her father snorted. "Nate wasn't smart enough to rob a convenience store without getting caught. Why would he try to kill you unless there was something in it for him?"

"Someone could have paid him to attack Kalea," Hawk reasoned.

Her father nodded. "Kalea, someone murdered him because he tried to kill you and failed." Her father raised his hands toward her. "Whoever is behind all these attempts is still out there."

"I can't hide away in the house. Who knows how long it will take to figure out who killed Nate?" Kalea took her father's hand. "I have to keep on living. Besides, if I hide, whoever is doing this will just wait until we think the threat is gone. As soon as I come out, he could be waiting." She turned to Hawk. "You hired Hawk to protect me. Let him do his job, and let me do mine. Maybe between the three of us, we can smoke out the killer sooner rather than later."

"I don't know," Hawk said. "Your father could be right. One person can't have a three-hundred-sixty-degree view of what's going on."

"You can't cover me in bubble wrap," Kalea protested. "I can't live like that."

"But I can't lose you," her father said. "You're all I have."

She squeezed his hand. "You're not going to lose me. Between Hawk and I, we'll manage. And maybe, getting away from the Big Island will take me away from the threat for a couple of days."

Her father's brow wrinkled. "You might have a point. All the attacks have been on this island. If you take our private plane, you're getting out before he can. He'd have to take commercial…assuming he doesn't have access to a private plane service." Her father nodded. "Leaving the island would give the police detectives more time to canvas the people surrounding Nate and find out who he's been in contact with."

Kalea let go of her father's hand. "So, I'm heading out to Oahu tomorrow as planned."

Her father nodded. "Maleko and I will come with you and Hawk to see you off."

Kalea smiled. "That would work." She tipped her head toward Hawk. "I'm going to change and get ready for my dance lesson with Lani. Tomorrow will be a long day of flying and meetings." Turning back to her father, she gave him a big hug. "I'm going to be all right. Hawk will take good care of me."

"He'd better," her father said. "I'm counting on him."

With her father calmed and her plan still in place, Kalea left the two men, climbed the stairs to her bedroom and stood staring at the walls without seeing them.

Nathaniel Bowman had been the man behind the attempts on her life. He was now dead...*murdered*. Possibly because he'd failed in his attempt to kill her. Who had killed Nate? Would that person now attempt to kill her himself?

CHAPTER 10

Hawk paced the length of porch, drinking in the balmy night air, searching for answers. After the ATV attack, he'd been nervous, afraid that by himself, he wasn't enough to keep Kalea safe. New to the task of being a bodyguard, he wondered if Patterson had chosen the right man for the job of protecting the ranch owner's only daughter.

He pulled his cellphone from his pocket. He'd tapped into the ranch's WIFI as soon as he'd arrived, giving him the connection he needed to contact his boss back in Montana. He dialed Patterson before he did the math, realizing that with a four hours' time difference the man might have already gone to bed.

"Hawk, I was just thinking about you," Patterson answered on the first ring.

"I didn't wake you up?" Hawk asked.

"No, I've been working online with Swede, going through the list of employees you gave me to work with. So far, nothing's popped up."

Hawk drew in a deep breath. "Well, things are getting a little crazy here."

"Tell me about it," Patterson said.

Hawk gave his boss the rundown on the ATV attack earlier that day and the subsequent murder of their attacker.

"Interesting," Patterson said. "I'm glad you two weren't hurt during the incident." He spoke in the background to someone with him. "I have Swede looking up Nathaniel Bowman now." He paused. "That was quick. Hang on…" There was more talking in the background that Hawk couldn't quite make out. Then Patterson came back. "The man has a history."

"That's what the police said."

"If he's dead, who killed him?" Patterson mused aloud. "And why?"

"I wish I knew." Hawk stared out at the stars shining over the pastures. "After Bowman tried to shoot us, I'm not feeling like I'm adequate coverage to protect Miss Parkman."

"I can send more Brotherhood Protectors your way. Hell, I can come myself."

"Give me a day. We're flying out to Oahu tomorrow. Hopefully, we won't run into the same issues there. We hope we leave them behind on the Big Island."

"I can be there within a day," Patterson said. "Just say the word."

"Thanks. I'm still new to this bodyguard gig. I liked it better when I knew who the enemy was."

"Me too, but even as SEALs, half the time we went into battle we didn't know who the bad guys were. We had to use our instincts and figure it out, sometimes with our fingers on the trigger."

"You're right. I guess it's not much different."

"Except you don't have a handgun or M4A1 rifle handy." Patterson laughed. "If I know you, you've got your Ka-Bar knife strapped somewhere on your body."

Hawk could feel the weight of his knife clipped to his belt. He patted it, glad for some kind of weapon to use against an unknown enemy. He hoped he discovered who it was before it was too late.

"Hawk?"

"Yeah."

"You know you can call me anytime, day or night."

"Yes, sir."

"I mean that. I'm here to help. We're still a team, even if you're a few thousand miles away."

"That's reassuring."

"We'll keep digging into backgrounds."

"Add another name to your list," Hawk said.

"Okay. Shoot."

"Tyler Beckett."

"Who is he to the Parkmans?" Patterson asked.

"The marketing lady, Clarise Sanders, brought him to dinner tonight. He wants to build a resort on Parkman Ranch."

"I thought Parkman Ranch was more into raising cattle than into tourism."

Hawk nodded, though Patterson couldn't see him. "Mr. Parkman prefers the cattle raising side of the business and just tolerates the minimal amount of tourism that goes on here. Miss Sanders wants him to consider expanding the tourism side of the corporation."

"And Parkman is against the idea?"

Hawk snorted. "Exactly."

"Then why did she bring Beckett to dinner?"

"I guess she's hoping to change Parkman's mind."

"I'll have Swede check into Beckett's background and let you know what we find." Patterson paused. "Remember, I can be there within a day."

"Thanks. I'll let you know how it goes in Honolulu. We're flying there tomorrow." Hawk ended the call and stepped down from the porch. With too much energy to relax, he needed to walk it off. He circled the perimeter of the house and outbuildings, pausing to peer into the distance. The stars shone brightly, lighting the sky and the ground below. Nothing appeared out of place or moved in the semi-darkness, except the horses in the fields.

One in particular came trotting up to the fence.

Hawk recognized Pain Killer as he stuck his nose over the fence and nuzzled Hawk's shoulder.

"I'm sorry. I don't have a carrot for you." He'd have to remember to bring a treat with him when he went for a walk near the pastures. Hawk reached out and rubbed the animal's velvety nose. "I see you made it back to the barn without incident. Thanks for leaving me stranded." And he meant it. If PK hadn't left him at the gate that afternoon, he wouldn't have been able to catch Kalea skinny-dipping in the pool. And he wouldn't have had her naked body pressed up against his in the water.

His groin tightened. How he wished he was back in the pool with the beautiful Hawaiian. She made his heart beat faster and blood burn through his veins. If the situation were any different, he'd ask her out.

"If wishes were horses…" he muttered the old quote his mother used to say when he wished for something other than what he had as a child.

He was Kalea's protector. Not her lover. Not her boyfriend or anything else. He needed to remember that.

With one last pat to the horse's nose, he turned back to the house. A light in a downstairs window drew his attention. As he neared the house, the melodic sound of Hawaiian music drifted through the open window.

A figure swayed in the light, a silhouette from the distance. But Hawk knew who it was before he could see her face. He moved closer until he stood below the porch, looking into the open window where Kalea practiced her native dance with Lani, her instructor.

Her arms and hips swayed to the gentle beat of the music, her hands flowing like flags in a breeze as she told a story through her movements.

Hawk couldn't move. He was captivated by her beauty and the loveliness of the sway of her hips and the tiny steps she took, turning around and back and forth. When the music ended, he stood still, staring at the woman in the window.

"I fell in love with her mother the first time I saw her dance," a voice said in the shadows.

Hawk dragged his gaze away from the amazing woman and looked up to where her father leaned against a pole on the deck. "I'm sorry. I shouldn't be gawking. It's just that I've never seen anyone dance quite like that."

John Parkman laughed. "It's mesmerizing. I think there's a little magic involved."

"She's beautiful," Hawk said, without thinking.

"Yes, she is. And I love her so very much." He sighed. "I can't imagine anyone wanting to hurt her."

"Do you have any enemies who want to get back at you for some slight?"

Mr. Parkman shook his head. "No. We keep our heads down and do what we do best."

"Raise cattle," Hawk finished for him.

"Besides, if someone was mad at me, why take it out on Kalea?"

"Because he knows she's the center of your universe." He lowered his voice. "Killing her would kill you."

Mr. Parkman drew in a shaky breath and let it out slowly. "How can I protect her? You've seen how independent she is. She won't let anyone confine her to four walls."

Hawk smiled. "No, she wouldn't tolerate it."

Kalea's father held out his hand. "Please, take good care of my daughter tomorrow."

Hawk shook the man's hand. "I'll do my best, sir." He prayed his best would be good enough.

THAT NIGHT, he slept fitfully, waking every hour. At one point, he rose from his bed, slipped out his door and peeked into Kalea's bedroom. She was sound asleep, her hand tucked beneath her cheek, her long dark hair fanned out on the white pillowcase. He wanted to go to her and hold her in his arms. He told himself it was to make sure no one else sneaked into her room, which was partly true. But the deeper reason was that once he'd held and kissed her, he knew he couldn't resist holding and kissing her again. How could he do his job when he couldn't take his eyes off the woman?

Hawk left his room well before dawn and walked the perimeter again. As the sun rose, he searched the surrounding area for places a sniper could perch and pick off anyone he pleased. The barn was the tallest building on the compound. He spent a few minutes searching the interior of the barn, coming up blessedly short of bad guys.

Maleko waylaid him as he exited the barn. "Is there something I can help you find?"

"No, thank you. I'm just familiarizing myself with the ranch."

Maleko tilted his head. "I understand you're flying with Miss Parkman to Oahu today."

Hawk nodded.

Maleko looked up at the clear morning sky. "You might not be back for a few days."

"We only planned on being gone, at the most, one night."

"The island spirits might say otherwise. A storm is brewing." Maleko moved past him to scoop a bucket of feed from a bin. "Plan on several days," he said over his shoulder.

Soft laughter sounded behind Hawk.

He turned to find Kalea standing behind him.

"Maleko's people have deep roots in the gods and deities of the Polynesian people. He believes the earth, ocean and skies are ruled by gods."

"Your people, too," Maleko said from where he poured feed into a trough in a stall.

Kalea nodded. "True. In this case, gods and the weatherman have given warning. A storm is brewing in the Pacific and is heading this direction. We should be back in plenty of time. But just in case, we should pack for a few days."

"Noted." He waited for Kalea to decide which direction she was headed.

"You don't have to hover. I'll be all right out here with Maleko. I want to brush *Pupule* before I leave him." She held up a handful of carrots. "Want one for PK?"

Hawk grinned. "As a matter of fact, I owe him. I disappointed him when I didn't have one on my walk last night."

"You went for a walk after I left you in the study?"

"I did."

Kalea handed him a carrot. "Did you discover anything new?"

He debated telling her he'd seen her dancing but decided that would be his little secret. She might think of him as a peeping Tom. "Nothing interesting."

Her mouth twisted. "Not even the fact you were watching me dance through the window?" She snorted softly. "Now, I'm disappointed—and don't bother offering me a carrot. It won't buy you forgiveness." She winked and walked away to *Pupule*'s stall.

Hawk chuckled and left the barn.

PK trotted over to him at the fence and took the offering, crunching loudly with his approval.

"What is it about women?" Hawk asked the horse. "You think you have them figured out, and then bam. You're clueless, again."

PK nodded his head in agreement.

Hawk returned to the barn, found a brush and stood on the other side of *Pupule*, brushing the horse with Kalea.

They worked in a companionable silence.

The earthy scent of horse manure and dust filled Hawk's senses, giving him a feeling of being at home. He could get used to working as a ranch hand in Hawaii. The Big Island had all the requisites with some added bonuses. Once his bodyguard duties were done, he might consider applying for the *paniolo* position with the Parkman Ranch. He'd work with the horses and cattle he loved, and during his time off, he could take up surfing and scuba diving off the coast. Another bonus was never having to ride out in minus forty-degree weather to check on the cattle during the dead of the winter.

Patterson would understand. Hell, if he wanted, he could work on the side as a Brotherhood Protector in Hawaii. He could open a whole new office on the islands. There were enough rich people who needed protection here. A lot more than were in Montana.

After the killer was apprehended and Kalea was safe, Hawk would bring up the subject with Patterson.

First things first. Eliminate the threat to Kalea.

He finished brushing his side at the same time as Kalea finished hers and looked over the horse's back. "When do we leave?"

"After breakfast." She took his brush, carried it into the tack room then led her horse out to the pasture. As soon as she released him, the horse trotted out a couple yards, laid down in a patch of dirt and rolled.

Hawk laughed.

Kalea shook her head. "I don't know why I bother." She turned and walked toward the house.

Hawk took her hand and held it all the way up the steps, not releasing it until he opened the back door.

She glanced down at their connected hands.

"Keeping up our cover," he explained.

She smiled and let go, passing him to enter the house.

Her father was already in the kitchen at the large table in the corner. He looked up from his plate with a forkful of fluffy scrambled eggs on his fork. "Sorry, I didn't wait. I was hungry."

"It's not like we're company," Kalea said. "We're going to wash our hands and be right back."

Hawk followed her to the powder room where they bumped into each other at the single sink.

He liked being close to her and liked it more when she pumped the liquid soap into his palm. Like the Hawaiian ranch, he could get used to having her around.

"Are you nervous about flying in a little plane to one of the other islands?" she asked.

"Not at all. I've been island hopping in Navy Ospreys and Army Black Hawk helicopters. If something goes wrong with the engine in a fixed wing aircraft, you have a better chance of survival."

She laughed and handed him the towel. "I try not to dwell on that, but you're right. And our aircraft is a sea plane."

"Even better, considering we're surrounded by water on all sides." He grinned, wiping his hands dry before following her back to the kitchen.

They joined Parkman and Ule at the table, discussing cattle, the weather and the meeting Kalea would attend in Honolulu later that afternoon.

"I heard from the police, they say they found a dark ski mask in Nate's apartment," her father said.

"That would explain who attacked me in Waimea," Kalea said. "Did you ask them if Nate had a snake tattoo on the back of his hand like the guy who attacked me in Hilo?"

Mr. Parkman shook his head. "I didn't, but I will."

After their meal, Kalea and Hawk hurried up the stairs to pack a bag for the trip.

Taking Maleko's prediction in mind, Hawk threw clothes for a few days, his toiletries and a handful of protein bars, in case they were too busy to stop for lunch or dinner, all into a backpack and slung it over his shoulder.

He met Kalea in the hallway. She carried a small roll-away suitcase and a backpack.

"Ready?" she asked.

He nodded.

Mr. Parkman and Maleko waited outside in a farm truck.

Hawk held open the back door for Kalea, waited for her to get in then closed it behind her. He hurried around to the other side and slipped in, dropping his bag to the floor.

The trip to the small Waimea airport took less than twenty minutes. When they arrived, the three men surrounded Kalea and walked with her to a Cessna seaplane parked in a hanger. A man driving a utility cart pulled the craft out of the hanger onto the tarmac.

Kalea thanked the man and walked around the exterior of the aircraft, looking at the wings, landing gear, ailerons and more.

Maleko carried her suitcase to the door and set it inside behind a passenger seat.

Hawk glanced around.

"Having a change of heart?" Mr. Parkman asked.

"Not at all. I was wondering when the pilot would show."

Parkman laughed out loud.

Hawk frowned. "What's so funny?"

Kalea stood in front of him, her fist on her hip. "You're looking at the pilot."

A slight sinking feeling hit the pit of Hawk's belly. "You're a pilot?"

Her lip curled up on one side. "What's the matter? Are you afraid a girl can't fly this plane?"

"No, not at all. I guess I have a lot more to learn

about you, Miss Parkman." He smiled and tossed his backpack into the plane.

"I guess so." Kalea waved a hand toward the plane. "This was my father's gift to me for my twenty-fifth birthday."

"Is that when you got your pilot's license?"

She laughed. "No. I've had it since my eighteenth birthday." Raising a brow, she faced him. "You can still change your mind about coming with me. I won't judge…much."

"No, no. I'm still committed to the trip," he said, wishing he sounded more convincing than he did. He shook Mr. Parkman's hand and then Maleko's. "We'll see you, hopefully, this afternoon."

"But don't be surprised if we take a little longer in Honolulu. You know how those tourism meetings can drag on," Kalea said.

"We could just shut down that portion of our business and skip all the ass-kissing," her father offered.

Kalea smiled. "So many people in this area rely on the Parkman Ranch experience for their livelihoods. We'd put all of them out of work."

Her father sighed. "We can't do that."

"No. So, I have to show up or we won't go into the tourism guide, and our employees will be out of work." She kissed her father's cheek. "See you soon. And don't worry. Hawk will take good care of me."

Her father pulled her into a tight hug. "I'm counting on it. Love you, girl."

"Love you, too, Daddy." She hugged Maleko.

He pointed to the sky to the southwest. "Get to

Oahu and stay until the storm clears. It's going to get here quicker than the weatherman said."

She nodded. "Thanks for the warning. You know me…I don't fly in unsafe conditions."

He patted her cheek. "You're a good pilot. Come home safely."

She kissed his cheek, climbed the steps and settled into the pilot's seat.

Hawk climbed in after her and closed the door behind him.

"Sorry, we don't have beverage service on this flight," Kalea said with a wink. "But we do have a safety briefing." She pointed out the features of the aircraft, the exit doors and the floatation devices required if they should have to bring the craft down over water. "This is a seaplane. If we have to land on water, we're equipped for that eventuality. I've done it a number of times. And don't worry, the annual service was performed less than a month ago. The plane was given an excellent bill of health." She put on her headset, checked the gauges, switched on the master switch and looked right then left. "Clear?"

Hawk looked around and nodded. "Clear." He slipped the co-pilot's headset over his ears and adjusted the microphone close to his mouth. "Just how many hours do you have flying?"

"A few."

"How many is a few?" Hawk asked, not feeling any less nervous about flying with the boss's daughter.

The engine roared to life, the noise almost drowning out her reply. "Hit the noise-cancelling button on your headset." Kalea pointed to the button and went through her pre-flight checklist. Then she keyed her mic and announced that she was taxiing out to the runway.

A couple minutes later, they were racing down that runway, gaining speed until Kalea pulled back on the yoke and the airplane left the ground and Hawk's stomach behind.

A chuckle sounded in his ear. "You can relax now. It's less than an hour to Honolulu. But first, I wanted you to see something." She turned the plane to the east, gaining altitude. "Below is the ranch, all 130,000 acres. We employ over 350 people. We have over 25,000 cattle and more than 800 miles of fence. The grassland is rich and year-round, unlike many places on the mainland."

Hawk looked out the window as they circled the massive spread. "It's an amazing operation. I can see why you love it."

"That's not why I brought you up here." She smiled and turned the plane toward Mauna Kea, the tallest mountain on the island. "You're familiar with Mauna Kea?"

He shrugged. "A little."

"There are thirteen observatories on Mauna Kea. Each one is sponsored by as many as eleven countries."

"I didn't know that."

She gave him a sideways glance. "I'll take you up there."

"Now?" Hawk asked.

Kalea laughed. "No. We'll drive up there some day. There isn't a safe place to land a plane up there. But that's not where we're going."

"I thought we were going to Oahu."

"We are, but on our way out, there's something else I want you to see." She flew the plane toward the northeastern coastline. The terrain became more tropical, the trees denser, the terrain rising higher as they approached the coast.

"Hold onto your hat," Kalea said into the mic.

"What?" Hawk gripped the armrest. "Why?"

Before he could guess what she was going to do, she pushed the yoke forward, diving down into a steep valley with waterfalls plunging thousands of feet to the valley floor.

"Sweet Jesus!" Hawk called out, now clinging to the armrest for dear life. "Pull up! Pull up!"

She did, leveling out several hundred feet below the tops of the ridges surrounding the ruggedly steep slopes. "This is the Kohala coastline with its thousands of waterfalls and beauty you can only see from the air." She shot a smile at him. "What's wrong? I thought you were used to flying. Hell, helicopters do crazier things than this."

"Yeah, but those pilots have hundreds of hours of flight experience under their belts."

Her grin broadened. "Trust me, so do I. I've been flying since I was sixteen. I've logged over a thousand hours, and I've flown this path at least fifty times. I wouldn't do anything that would put either one of us at risk."

"I'm glad to know that...now." He shook his head, his pulse rate slowly returning to normal. "Is this how you initiate all your *paniolos*?"

She flew to the end of the valley where it opened out to the ocean. "No. You're the first *paniolo* I've brought up with me in the plane. The only other passengers I've taken up are my father and Maleko."

"That's it? In all those hours?" He stared across at her. "Unless they flew in the military, the only other pilots I've known with that many hours were flight instructors."

She shrugged. "I can see a lot more of the ranch from up in the air. I go up at least once a week, sometimes more often, depending on what's going on."

As they cleared the cliffs, Kalea angled the plane to the northwest.

"The island you can see ahead is Maui. We won't fly over it, but we will fly over Kaho'olawe, a much smaller, deserted island that has been turned into a reserve. It was once used by the US military for bombing practice. They turned it over to the Hawaiian government in the early 1990s. The only people allowed on the island are volunteers who are there to help restore the island.

As they neared Kaho'olawe, Kalea descended so that they could get a better view of the island that had been ravaged by bombs. As the plane grew closer to the ground, the engine coughed, sputtered and died.

Kalea frowned.

"Was that supposed to happen?" Hawk asked.

"No," Kalea checked the gauges, turned on the fuel boost pump and cursed when nothing happened. "You know all those safety instructions I gave you before we took off?"

Hawk swallowed hard, his pulse picking up. "Yeah, why?"

"Looks like we might get to exercise some of them. Prepare for an emergency landing." She glanced out the window toward the larger island to the east. "We don't have enough altitude to coast into Maui. We'll be landing here, on or near Kaho'olawe."

CHAPTER 11

"THIS ISN'T another chance to fool the new guy, is it?" Hawk said. "Because, if it is, you got me. Now, turn the engine back on." He gave Kalea a weak smile, his hand curled tight around the armrest. "This isn't a drill, is it?"

She shook her head, looking out the window. "There isn't a landing strip on the island, so we'll be making a water landing. We need a long enough cove where the water is pretty smooth. We don't want to catch a wave. It could flip the plane."

"Now, I remember why I like helicopters," Hawk said, gripping the armrest.

Kalea snorted. "If a helicopter engine cuts out, it drops like a rock. Fixed wing aircraft can glide for miles. Now help me look for a cove. Preferably one with a beach we can get out on." Her voice was strained, her concentration on the terrain and coastline below.

Hawk peered out of the plane at the ground below, searching for the tell-tale light color of sand along the coastline and a cove big enough to land the plane without crashing into cliffs.

"There," he said, pointing toward a long crescent-shaped cove where the waves didn't crest as they gently slid onto the sandy shore. "Is there enough room for you to put the plane down?"

She nodded. "I think so. We're already going pretty slow. We just have to come at it from the correct angle and hope there isn't a lot of crosswind pushing us into the shore too soon."

Kalea swung out away from land and turned as the plane dropped lower, closer to the water. She adjusted the flaps, and then gripped the yoke, her feet pressing the pedals on the floor as she brought the aircraft down as slowly as she could. At the last minute, she pulled back on the yoke. The floats kissed the water then settled in the gentle surf, coming to a halt well before the other end of the cove where the cliffs rose up out of the water.

Hawk let go of the breath he'd been holding and turned to Kalea. "I take back all the bad things I was thinking back along the Kohala coastline. And it might be too soon in our relationship, but I think I'm in love." He reached across, gripped her cheeks between his palms and leaned close to try and kiss her. Their microphones bumped against each other.

Kalea laughed, pushed hers aside and his, and then kissed him. "I have to admit, in all the hours I've flown, I've never had an emergency landing. That was a first for me."

He shook his head. "And you were so cool and calm."

She reached for the radio, turned to the emergency frequency and pressed the mic key. "Mayday, mayday, mayday." She waited for a response. When no one came back to her, she frowned, turned the knob and listed. No crackling sounds of static, or anything sound for that matter, came through the headsets. "The radio is out."

"Won't the ATC send a search plane out when you don't show up in Honolulu?"

"No one knows I'm coming. I didn't file a flight plan. We didn't want anyone to know we were flying and give the killer notice we were leaving the island." She stared across at Hawk. "We might be here a while until my father realizes we didn't check in."

"At what point might that be?" Hawk asked.

"He might not worry until after the meetings were to take place."

"That would be later tonight." Hawk looked out the window at the clouds gathering to the southwest. "Maleko called it."

"How so?"

"He told me to pack for a few days. What he didn't say was to pack in food and drink for that many days."

"If we aren't discovered for a few days, we have another problem."

"As if we didn't have enough already," Hawk muttered. "What else?"

"This island doesn't have a fresh water source." She looked around in the back of the plane. "I usually leave a couple of bottles of water in the plane. But the last time I flew, I used one." She unbuckled her seatbelt. "We'd better get moving before the storm hits. I don't want to leave my plane in the water. I'd like to drag it to shore, if at all possible, and tie it down."

"Let's do this. I mean how long could it take someone to figure out we're stranded and come looking for us?"

"Hopefully not long. The weatherman did say the storm heading our way might last a couple of days. But even then, a boat from Maui could get here if the seas aren't too rough. The coastguard helicopters could find us and notify the shore patrol to come pick us up."

"I love your optimism." Hawk grinned. "But just in case, let's get what we need off the plane and pull the plane up on shore. I saw what appeared to be dirt roads leading up to a building a little farther inland. The plane is pretty small, we might want to consider sheltering from the storm in the building."

The storm the weatherman had said wouldn't arrive until later that evening had picked up steam and was bearing down on the island like a freight train on a downhill run. The clouds thickened, turning an angry shade of gray.

Hawk stripped out of his shirt, shoes and trousers and stuffed them into the backpack along with the rest of his clothes.

"What are you doing?" she asked, her eyebrows rising.

"Getting ready to swim the plane in. Is there a tie-down line?"

"Yeah. Let me get it." Kalea climbed out onto the one of the floats and worked her way around to the storage compartment while the little plane rocked on the waves that were getting bigger the closer the storm moved. She removed the line from the compartment and tied it to a metal loop on one of the floats.

Hawk dropped down onto the float beside her.

She handed the line to him and climbed back into the plane.

Hawk dove into the water.

A moment later, Kalea dove in beside him. When she surfaced, she wore only her bra and panties. "It will probably take the two of us to drag the plane ashore."

With both of them pulling on the line, they swam and tugged the plane through the water and tide until they made it to shore. Once they had their feet in the sand, they leaned back in an intense tug-of-war, between themselves and the sea, to get the plane as far up on the shore as they could.

Breathing hard and tired, they tied the plane to a rock and sank to their knees in the sand.

"At least, the tide is in. Hopefully, it won't go much higher, even with the storm kicking up waves." Hawk pushed to his feet and walked in his boxer briefs to the plane. There, he unloaded his backpack, dressed in shorts and a T-shirt and pulled his shoes on his feet.

Kalea appeared beside him. "Where do you get all that energy?" she grumbled. The wind had already begun to dry her hair. Strands whipped around her face. She pushed it behind her ears and turned to the plane.

"Do you want your backpack and your suitcase?"

She shook her head. "The suitcase can stay. I'll need my backpack and my clothes."

He handed her the shirt, trousers and low-heeled shoes she'd worn on the flight. While she dressed, he slung their backpacks over his shoulder and hiked to the edge of the little beach. From the air, he'd noticed a faded dirt road leading up the hill to an old abandoned building. They could hole up there, until the storm passed.

Kalea joined him, and they headed up the hill, finding the dirt road as they moved through low-lying scrub.

"I don't understand why the engine cut out," she said, chewing her bottom lip. "The annual came back clean, and I did the usual preflight checks before we got in. All I can figure is something contaminated the fuel. But that doesn't explain why the radio stopped working."

"Who knew we were flying out today besides your father, Maleko and me?"

Kalea shook her head. "Did we mention it when Clarise and Beckett were there at dinner?"

Hawk frowned. "Beckett mentioned that you were going to the Tourism Commission meeting today. Both he and Miss Sanders knew you were coming."

Kalea's brow dipped into a V. "You don't think either one of them might have sabotaged my plane, do you?"

Pushing his hand through his hair, Hawk shrugged. "I don't know, but who else would have known you were going, other than the people at the little airport when you called to have them pull the plane out?"

"I trust the people at the airport. It's so small. Everyone knows everyone. So many of the people in

Waimea depend on Parkman Ranch for their livelihoods," Kalea looked toward Hawk, her gaze troubled. "Why would they want to hurt a Parkman?"

"Jealousy? Anger over rich versus poor? There could be any number of reasons." Hawk looked around at the semi-desolate island. "Has your father fired anyone lately?'

"No."

"Did Nate ever work for your father?"

"No," Kalea came to a stop at a fork in the dirt road. "None of this is making any sense."

Hawk steered her left and continued walking. "What would Beckett or Miss Sanders gain if you died?"

"I can't imagine," Kalea said. "My father isn't going to change his mind about the resort, whether I live or die."

"What about Miss Sanders kissing your father's cheek last night?"

"What about it?"

"Is she interested in your father?"

Kalea shrugged. "I think so."

"Does she see you as a threat? Or maybe someone standing in her way of making a move on dear old dad?"

Kalea's brow knit. "My dad isn't old. And I'm not standing in the way of my father falling in love again. I want him to be happy."

Hawk raised his hands. "Just trying to work through the possibilities. I'm not saying anything, just playing devil's advocate."

"Clarise has been spending an inordinate amount of time at the ranch lately," she said slowly.

"Does she need to work at the ranch for her marketing position?"

Kalea shook her head. "Not really. She has an office in Waimea."

"For an employee, she was very cozy with your father, and she made plans with your chef as if she had the right to do so," Hawk pointed out.

"She can be pushy, but I don't like playing the hostess gig, so I don't mind." Kalea's lips twisted thoughtfully. "And Dad didn't seem to mind. But she wasn't the one who attacked me in the parking lots at Hilo or Waimea."

Hawk shifted the backpacks on his shoulder. "She could have hired Nate to do that."

"Come to think of it, Nate isn't as tall as the guy who attacked me at the hardware store in Hilo. However, he could have been the one who tried to get to me in Waimea, and he was the one on the ATV." She shot another glance at Hawk. "Could there be more than one guy out there gunning for me?"

Hawk didn't like seeing her confidence fade. He slipped an arm around her and brought her to a halt. "Hey, stick with me. I'll do my best to keep you safe."

She leaned into him briefly. "I can't imagine what I would have done if I'd been out riding alone when Nate attacked on his ATV." She laughed, though it sounded shaky. "You were amazing, grabbing him as he tried to run you over."

"I got lucky," Hawk said, his jaw tightening. "He could have killed us both."

She grabbed his arm, forcing him to stop and look at

her. "But he didn't. For that I'm thankful." She leaned up on her toes and pressed her lips to his. "Thank you."

Hawk pulled her into his arms and crushed her to his chest, his mouth descending to claim hers in a much longer, more thorough kiss. When he set her back on her feet, he lifted his head and stared down into her eyes. "Thank you for delivering us safely to this island. I'm in awe of your flying skills."

She laughed and leaned into him. "Don't thank me until we're rescued from this pile of rocks."

He took her hand and held it the rest of the way to the building he'd seen from the sky. After a couple near-death experiences with the beautiful Hawaiian, Hawk couldn't think of anything he'd rather be doing than holding her hand and being with her.

Unless being with her in a different location was an option.

CHAPTER 12

KALEA WAS glad for the hand holding hers. With the sky darkening to a wicked shade of steel gray, she was concerned for their safety. The last she'd heard on the weather report was that the storm was building and could reach cyclone status. And it was headed straight for the Hawaiian Islands.

Kaho'olawe was light on vegetation, relying mostly on rain to sustain itself. The few buildings on the island had been erected during World War II and had weathered many storms, but there had been little maintenance following each storm. Would the building they were heading toward be sufficient shelter from the storm or be made dangerous by flying debris?

Kalea held onto Hawk's hand and prayed to Kanaloa, god of the ocean; Kane, the god of the sky; and Lono, god of rain, for a safe journey through the path of the storm. What happened would happen. Then she prayed to the Christian God to deliver them safely back home.

A gray, weathered building made of tin appeared

ahead as the wind picked up and pushed them forward, as if hurrying them toward the shelter.

Hawk stopped outside the building, studying its structure and integrity with a frown. The tin roof flapped on one corner with every gust of wind. Other than that, the rest of the building seemed sturdy enough.

"I'll see what I can find in the way of a nail and hammer to secure that sheet of tin."

"I'd rather you didn't climb up on the roof in this wind," Kalea said.

"I'll be careful not to fall off and leave you stranded, caring for a man with a broken neck." He winked. "Let's see if we can get inside." He reached for the doorknob and turned it.

The handle didn't budge. "Okay. Let's see if there's another entrance. You want to stay here or go with me around the hut?"

"I'll go with you." She wasn't ready to release his hand, liking the feel of his strength wrapped around her fingers.

After a quick walk around the rectangular building, they determined the only door in or out was the one in front.

Kalea searched the area around the door for a potentially, hidden key. With no flowerpot or doormat to look beneath, she ran out of options pretty quickly. "We have a building, but we can't get inside," she said. "Guess we'll get wet in the storm."

"Not if I have anything to say about it." Hawk released her hand, set her away from the door then kicked it hard. The doorframe split, and the door slammed open.

"That's one way to do it," Kalea said with a crooked smile.

Hawk stepped through the doorframe and was swallowed by the dark interior. What few windows the building boasted were covered in a thick layer of salty grime that barely allowed light to shine through them.

Not wanting to let Hawk out of her sight, Kalea stepped in behind him and let her eyes adjust to the gloom.

The room appeared to have been some kind of barracks with metal bunk racks lined up on either side of the space for the length of the building. Old black and white striped mattresses were folded up at one end of the lower bunks.

"Looks like these have been used recently."

"They have volunteers come out periodically to help maintain the old buildings, plant native vegetations and weed out invasive species." Kalea looked around the sparsely furnished living quarters. "They usually stay on the other side of the island, but probably use these quarters when their work brings them this far over."

"We can make it work."

"Now, if only we could find some food stashed away in a pantry, or something." Kalea rubbed her flat belly. "Otherwise, we'll get hungry before they send the Coast Guard to rescue us."

"I have a handful of protein bars we can munch on. That will hold us over until help arrives." He laid his backpack on a bunk. "I think I'd rather sleep on the floor. These bunks don't look very sturdy."

"We can stack the mattresses and make a pallet on the floor," Kalea suggested. "I have a beach blanket back in the plane we can use to spread over the mattresses."

The wail of the wind blowing through the cracks in the walls increased as the storm neared the islands.

"Good idea," Hawk said. "I'll go back and get the blanket."

"I'll start stacking the mattresses." Kalea gathered a thin mattress from one of the bunks and spread it out on the floor.

"The blanket can wait. Those mattresses look heavy," Hawk said and grabbed one from a bunk, laying it out next to the one Kalea has already positioned. Soon, they had the mattresses stacked three deep.

"We'd better go get that blanket before the storm hits," Kalea said. "I'm coming with you."

Knowing the way and traveling downhill made it faster getting back to the plane. Kalea did her best to keep up with Hawk, refusing to slow him down. She considered herself in pretty good shape, but Hawk had her beat by a mile.

The wind had picked up considerably since they'd landed, causing whitecapped waves on the ocean, and driving them into the shore. Thankfully, they'd pulled the plane up far enough on the sand to keep the waves from dragging it back into the water.

"I'm glad we landed when we did," Kalea said as she climbed up into the plane, found the blanket and handed it out to Hawk. "I couldn't have landed in this."

"I'm glad we did, too. Hopefully, the storm won't last long."

Kalea didn't respond to his comment. Was it wrong of her to want the storm to last a couple of days? Then she could be alone with Hawk, with no one judging or interrupting their time together. She liked the man and admired his dedication to protecting her.

Was his attraction to her purely part of the act? Or was he just trying to make the client happy? Kalea preferred to think he really found her irresistible and worthy of his kisses.

Once again, they held hands all the way back to the building.

Inside, they spread the blanket over the stacks of mattresses and settled onto them with their backpacks to inventory what they'd managed to bring for sustenance.

Kalea smiled as she pulled out a brown paper bag. "I could kiss Maleko," she said.

Hawk frowned. "Do you kiss all your employees?"

She gave him a sassy flip of her hair. "You'd think I did, based on the number of times I've kissed you." Kalea held up the bag. "Maleko doesn't like it when I eat fast food. Whenever I travel to Oahu, he packs a bag full of sandwiches and veggie snacks." She opened the bag and peeked inside. "He packed enough for both of us. Two sandwiches each." Digging around again, she unearthed a flashlight and set it in the middle of the floor. "We can use this later when the night really settles in. But for now, are you hungry? Would you like a sandwich?"

"I am," Hawk said. "But let's bank on a longer lead time for our rescue and eat only half a sandwich. We can save the other half for dinner."

"Good point." She opened the wrapper and handed a neatly cut half of a sandwich to him, taking the other for herself. "Mmm. Chicken sandwich. Must have had some leftovers from dinner last night." She took a bite and chewed thoughtfully. "So, what do you want to do for the next few hours until night? I have a deck of cards I keep to play solitaire when I'm alone. We can play rummy."

"Sounds good. *After* I repair the roof tin. But I have to warn you. I'm amazing at cards." He winked and bit into his sandwich.

Kalea liked it when he flirted with her and smiled as she finished her sandwich, sipped water from the only water bottle they'd brought from the plane, and then pulled out the deck of worn playing cards. She set it aside and went out of the building to watch as Hawk climbed up onto the roof with a rock and a nail he'd found in a cabinet drawer. After he banged the nail into the tin to hold down the corrugated sheet of roofing metal, he slid off the edge of the roof and landed on the ground beside her. She wrapped her arms around him until he was steady on his feet.

"Thanks. You know you're pretty handy to have around." He bent and kissed the tip of her nose. Then he pulled her against him and kissed her lips in a long, passionate kiss, leaving Kalea's head spinning when he finally came up for air.

"What was that for?" she asked, her voice barely audible over the wailing of the wind.

"Just because. When we get back to the ranch, I probably won't get to do that again. Hell, I shouldn't have done it now. But what do you expect from a man stranded on a deserted island with a beautiful woman?"

They played rummy for the next couple of hours as the storm surrounded them. The clouds thickened and blocked out the daylight, making it as dark as the darkest night, hours before the official sunset.

The storm raged outside the building, rattling the tin roof. Kalea was thankful Hawk had nailed the loose tin before the storm hit. At least the rain wasn't coming through the ceiling.

Too dark to play cards, Kalea used the flashlight like a candle for them to eat their dinner by. Each had half a sandwich and half a candy bar for dessert. They drank from the water bottle and capped the remainder for the next day.

With nothing else to do, and wanting to conserve the battery, they decided to turn off the flashlight and try to sleep.

The only time they could see anything was when lightning lit the sky. For a while, that was every five or ten minutes as the storm passed overhead.

"Pele must be angry," Kalea murmured in the darkness following the lightning.

"Pele?"

"The goddess of wind, fire and lightning." A rumble of thunder shook the building.

Hawk chuckled. "She's definitely making her voice heard."

Kalea shivered and moved closer to Hawk, laying her head in the crook of his arm.

He held her close. "Scared?"

"Not of the storm."

He shifted. "Are you afraid of me?"

She shook her head against his chest. "No. I think I'm more afraid of myself."

"How so?" He rested his lips against her hair, his breath warm on her scalp.

"I'm becoming far too dependent on you."

"Only until we figure out who's after you."

She laid her hand across his chest. "Not dependent on your protection, although I do appreciate it."

"I don't understand," he said, turning her to face him.

A flash of lightning revealed he was looking at her. And after a brief second, all went black again.

Could he see what was in her eyes? Could he tell that she was falling for him?

"Never mind." She snuggled closer to him, enjoying every second of the time she had left with him. They could figure out who her attacker was tomorrow, arrest the man and Hawk could be on his way back to Montana.

Her throat tightened, and her eyes burned. A single tear found its way out of the corner of her eye.

At that exact moment, another flash of lightning illuminated the room.

Hawk frowned. "Is that…?"

Darkness.

"—a tear?" he asked softly.

"I don't know what you're talking about," she said, quickly wiping away the evidence. But another popped up behind the first and slipped down her cheek.

"Why are you crying?"

"I don't know," she whispered.

"If I could, I'd get you back home right this minute," he said. "But for now, we're going to be all right. The storm will pass soon, and we'll be rescued."

"I know that," she said. "I'm not worried about that."

He touched a finger to her chin and lifted it. "Then why are you sad?"

"It doesn't matter," she said and pressed his palm to her cheek. "We're here now. We should sleep." She turned her face and kissed his palm.

Hawk found her lips in the darkness and captured them with his own. "I can't think of anyone I'd rather be stranded with on a deserted island."

"I know you're being paid to look out for me. You don't have to say nice things."

He chuckled. "Okay. Then I quit." Again, he pressed his lips to hers. "Ah...that's much better."

Kalea laughed. "You're crazy."

"No, really. I'm not working for your father anymore. I'm under no obligation to be nice to you. And best of all...you're not my client. I can kiss you without breaking any rules." To prove it, he kissed her again.

Kalea wrapped her arms around his neck and pulled him closer, opening to him, thrusting her tongue past his lips to tangle with his. She pressed her breasts to his chest, her hips to his hips and felt the hard ridge of his erection nudging against her belly.

Again, lightning lit the sky. An answering jolt of electricity ripped through Kalea's veins, shooting downward to coil at her core. She couldn't get close enough to this man. Finding the hem of his shirt, she pushed it up his torso.

His hand covered hers and halted her progress. "If we start this, I can't promise I can stop."

"Please," she said. "I don't want you to stop. I want you. Now." He moved his hand, and she pushed up the shirt, drew it over his head and dropped it on the blanket beside them.

Then she grabbed the hem of her shirt and yanked it up her body.

"Hey, that's my job," he said and took over, dragging it slowly over her skin, following it with his lips, touching the skin he bared as he went.

Kalea was on fire, the heat building like lava trapped inside a volcano, compressing until it could force its way free. Her hands found the button on his jeans and flicked it free. She slid his zipper downward until his shaft sprang free into her palm.

He was hard, thick and pulsing with energy.

He groaned. "Sweetheart, you're killing me."

"Then we will die together," she said.

Hawk reached behind her and unclipped her bra, sliding the straps over her shoulders and down her arms.

Kalea threw back her head and drew short, shallow

breaths, finding it difficult to breathe, she was so affected by his hands on her naked skin.

He bent to take one of her nipples between his lips, rolling it on his tongue, and then nipping the tip.

Her core spasmed, and she arched her back, urging him to take more.

Sucking her breast into his mouth, he pulled hard then left it to treat the other to the same pleasurable pull.

By then, Kalea could barely catch her breath. She reached down to unhook the catch on her trousers. Again, Hawk's hand covered hers and stopped her before she could get started.

"Let me," he said, his mouth touching the sensitive spot below her earlobe. Then he kissed the length of her throat, traveling over her collarbone to the swell of her breast. He didn't stop there, searing a path over each of her ribs until he found his way to the waistband of her trousers.

He paused long enough to unhook the metal clasp on her trousers and slid the zipper down.

Kalea bucked beneath him. "Too slow," she moaned.

He chuckled and dragged her trousers over her hips. "Better."

"Yes," she said on a sigh, counting the seconds until he finally pulled the pants all the way off her legs.

Then he slipped his fingers beneath the elastic of her panties and cupped her sex.

Kalea thought she was going to die right then and there. How much longer would she have to wait to have all of him inside her?

CHAPTER 13

A FLASH of lightning illuminated Kalea's face as Hawk hovered over her, his finger slipping into her channel. "So wet. So very wet," he said and leaned up to kiss her lips.

He couldn't help himself. She was amazing, both in body and spirit. He'd never met anyone quite like Kalea. He could fall in love with this woman, if he hadn't already.

He set about pleasing her first before slaking his own desires. He followed the same path down her body as before, moving quickly to the sweet spot between her legs. There he paused, his breath stirring the curls covering her sex.

She quivered beneath him, a moan sounding in the silence between roars of thunder. Her body tensed beneath him, as if waiting to see if he'd go that one step further.

And he did.

Parting her folds, he bent to touch the tip of his tongue to the strip of flesh packing myriad nerves.

Kalea arched off the mattress, her fingers threading into his hair, digging into his scalp. "Yes!"

He chuckled and flicked that nubbin, sending her into another spasm. Then he sucked that button of flesh into his mouth and twirled it around with the tip of his tongue, flicking and licking until Kalea dug her heels into the blanket and pulled on his hair as her body quaked with her release.

He kissed her there and thrust a finger inside her, swirling around, loving how damp she was and ready.

"Now," she said on a gasp. "I need you inside me. Now."

He dug into his back pocket and pulled out his wallet, fumbling in the dark until he found what he was searching for. When he did, he dropped the wallet, tore open the foil packet and applied the protection over his straining cock. With his jeans pushed down around his hips, he lay down between her legs, his staff poised at her entrance. "Tell me what you want," he said, pressing a kiss to the pulse beating so wildly against the base of her throat.

"You. I want you," she cried. Kalea gripped his hips in her hands and brought him home.

He slid inside, her channel convulsing around him, pulling him deeper. Easing in slowly, he allowed her time to adjust to his girth before going all the way. When he was as deep as he could go, he paused. "Okay?"

"More than okay," she said. She pushed his hips away, stopping before he completely disengaged and brought him close again. In and out, she set the pace, starting slow and increasing the strokes, moving faster and faster until Hawk took over.

By then, he'd gone past control and thrust again and again, the tension building, adrenaline roaring through his veins, and ripples of electricity shooting outward from their intimate connection, all the way to his fingers and toes.

He thrust once more and buried himself deep inside her, holding steady, until the tremors ebbed, and he could once again draw a breath into his lungs.

Hawk collapsed over her and rolled her onto her side, facing him, maintaining their hold on one another. He smoothed a strand of her hair away from her cheek. "I wish I could see you. I can't tell what you're thinking." Suddenly, he was nervous, wondering if he'd pushed her too fast. "Was this too soon? Did I hurt you? Talk to me, Kalea."

"You should have quit before we kissed in the pool at the ranch. Now, I'm imagining what we missed," she said on a sigh. Her hand slipped up his arm, feeling along his neck until she cupped his cheek in her hand. "I've never felt quite so…satiated." She followed her hand to his mouth and pressed her lips to his.

Hawk released the breath he'd been holding and kissed her back, holding her close, loving the way he felt inside her.

As the storm raged around the building, Hawk hugged Kalea close. Eventually, the thunder moved on, the winds died down, and they fell asleep in each other's arms.

. . .

DULL GRAY LIGHT edged through the grimy windows, waking Hawk in the early hours of the morning.

Kalea slept on, curled on her side against him, her hand tucked beneath her chin.

Needing to relieve himself, Hawk gently extricated himself from Kalea's arms and legs and rolled off the pallet and up onto his feet. Quickly dressing, he pulled on his shoes, strapped his knife to his calf and eased the door open.

Outside, the scent of freshly washed earth and vegetation filled the air. Gulls flew overhead, and the sky, though cloudy, wasn't nearly as threatening as it had been the night before.

Hawk visited the outhouse he'd found behind the building and relieved himself. Curious about the plane, and knowing Kalea would be worried about it, he hurried down to the cove.

Before he reached the sand, his heart sank. The plane that had been well over the sand was gone.

Hawk looked out to sea, but the little Cessna seaplane was nowhere to be seen. He dropped down to the sand and went to where they'd tied the plane to a rock. Still tied to the rock was line they'd used. Only it appeared to have been cut, not torn or frayed.

With a frown. Hawk looked up again and around the sandy shore to the opposite end of the long strip of sand. That's when he saw it. A small motorboat was pulled up on the sand, half-hidden behind a boulder.

His first instinct was to be glad someone had come

to rescue them. But immediately following that thought was the image of the line cut in two. The line that had secured Kalea's plane to the shore.

As if drawn to it, Hawk crossed the stretch of sand, walking...then running toward the small boat. As he neared the craft, he realized it didn't belong to the coast guard, and it didn't have any markings on it to identify it.

Pulling his knife from the scabbard around his calf, he edged closer. Footprints disturbed the sand all around the boat and back toward the boulder where the plane had been secured.

But there was no sign of a person.

A cold feeling settled in the pit of Hawk's gut.

Whoever had come ashore had cut the plane free and pushed it out into the ocean. He had to have been there for long enough to do that and possibly long enough to find his way up to—

Hawk swore, turned and ran across the sand as fast as his feet could carry him. He cursed how the loose sand made it more difficult for him to gain traction. When he reached the hard-packed dirt and old road, he sprinted, moving as fast as he could. He had to get back to the building...to Kalea...before...

KALEA WOKE when the door to the building closed behind Hawk. She smiled and stretched, feeling good despite being stranded on an island with no running water for a shower or to brush her teeth. She was sore, but in a good way. She wouldn't mind waking up that way every day. But preferably with Hawk still in the bed beside her.

When he didn't return right away, Kalea figured he'd gone down to check on the plane. She rose and dressed, eager to see how her Cessna had weathered the wicked storm the night before.

Having just pulled on her shoes and finger-combed her hair, she heard a sound outside the door. With a smile on her face, she hurried to greet the man who'd shown her how beautiful lovemaking could be when you did it with the right person. She flung open the door and started to throw herself into his arms, when she realized the man in front of her wasn't Hawk at all.

He was tall and stocky, and his face appeared as if set in granite.

Without thinking, Kalea blurted out, "You're not Hawk." Then her brow furrowed. "Who are you? And where is Hawk?"

The man didn't say anything, just reached out and grabbed for her arm.

Kalea jerked away, stepping backward into the building. That's when she saw the tattoo on the back of the man's hand—the snake she'd seen on her attacker's hand in Hilo.

Her heart leaped into her throat, and she quickly weighed her options. She could try to plough right through him and escape or run back into the building and evade him long enough for Hawk to return and help her get this guy under control.

Knowing she wouldn't make it past him through the

door, Kalea chose option two and backed another step into the building.

When the man in the doorway moved, Kalea turned and ran.

She didn't get far before a hand grabbed her hair, and she was yanked backward. Stumbling, she fell hard on her hip. But that hand in her hair kept her from shaking loose from her attacker.

He pulled her to her feet and wrapped a steel band of an arm around her middle and walked with her toward the door.

"What do you want? If it's money, my father will pay you anything you want if you don't kill me."

"I'm not interested in your father's money," he said, his voice low and gravelly.

"Were you the one who killed Nate? I know you were the one in Hilo wearing the Phantom mask. You know you're not going to get away with anything, don't you? No one ever does. Eventually, you'll be caught. Hopefully, sooner than later." Kalea knew she was babbling, but she was trying to keep him talking to allow Hawk time to get back to her. Assuming the man holding her hadn't killed the Navy SEAL.

No, he couldn't have killed her man. Hawk had promised she'd be okay. He would stake his life on it. Kalea prayed he hadn't given his life to save hers. If he had, she wasn't so sure she wanted to continue living. She wanted more time with the man. He intrigued her and made her want to be with him every minute of every day. He couldn't be dead.

Something cold and hard pressed against her

temple. Out of the corner of her eye, she recognized the black barrel and handgrip of a pistol. "Are you going to shoot me?" she asked, her pulse pounding, her stomach roiling.

"Not yet. First, I have to get your boyfriend out in the open," he said.

A mixture of relief and fear warred inside Kalea. Relief that her captor hadn't found Hawk yet. And fear that using her as a bargaining chip to bring out Hawk would expose him to the lethal force of a man with a gun. "He's not my boyfriend," she said, while wishing Hawk actually was. The fleeting thought flashed through her mind, *Just what are we?* They'd slept together, made love and then what? Were they lovers or a one-night stand?

"What are you going to do when he does come out in the open?" Kalea asked. "You don't want to kill us. You'll go to jail for the rest of your life. I hear jail in Hawaii is horrible. You're so close to the beaches, but you'll never see them again."

"Shut up," the man said through gritted teeth. "You talk too much."

"I only talk like this when I'm nervous. You'd be nervous, too, if you had a gun pointing at your head. It's not every day you have a gun pointed at your head. You really don't want to shoot me. It would make a very big mess."

"Then I guess I'll have to drown you to make you shut up," he said and jabbed her with the tip of the barrel. "Shut your pie hole, lady. Your man should be showing up soon. Then we can start this party."

"So, we're going to have a party?" A movement out of the corner of Kalea's eyes caught her attention. She could see Hawk peering through the bushes toward her. He lifted a finger to his mouth.

Afraid her captor would turn that gun on Hawk, Kalea preferred that he shoot her instead. She kept up her running diatribe, hoping she would come up with a way to get out of her captor's grip at the same time as she could disarm him. But he had a tight hold around her middle, and her arms were pinned to her sides. "So, why are you set on killing me and my ranch hand?" she asked.

"That's my business," he said. "I told you to shut up."

"You're going to kill us anyway, so what's it hurt to tell me why? You wouldn't want me to go to my grave with such a big question weighing my spirit down, would you?"

"I don't give a rat's ass about your spirit. If you don't shut up, I'll make you shut up."

"If you kill me before my ranch hand appears, he'll kill you. You can't kill me yet."

"Don't tempt me," he said. "All I have to do is apply pressure here…" he said, shifting the arm holding the gun from pointing it at her head and wrapping it around her throat. "And then squeeze. You won't be able to breathe and, eventually, you'll pass out. Maybe even die. Which is why I'm here on this godforsaken lump of rock." He squeezed gently, cutting off the air Kalea fought hard to fill her lungs. With her hands trapped at her sides, she could only kick her feet and twist her body in an attempt to break free and suck in life-giving air.

Her captor was stronger, holding her down, keeping her from moving.

Soon, the sunshine faded to a fuzzy gray and, finally, to black.

CHAPTER 14

HAWK LAY in the brush several yards away from where a man with a snake tattoo on his hand held a gun to Kalea's temple. He refused to show himself. If he did, he was certain Kalea's captor would shoot without giving him any chance to run. If he died, he wouldn't be able to save Kalea.

When her captor wrapped his arm around Kalea's throat, Hawk knew he had to do something, and do it quickly. He wished he had a rifle, but he didn't. Armed with nothing more than a knife, he had to do whatever he could.

Ka-Bar knife in hand, he waited, praying for a chance. He inched closer, low crawling toward the man choking the life out of the woman he couldn't get out of his mind. He prayed he wasn't too late when he was finally able to make his move.

Kalea's body went limp. When it did, she slipped through her captor's arm toward the ground.

The man bent to keep her from falling but couldn't juggle her and the gun in his hand.

Clutching his Ka-Bar, Hawk waited for the moment when Kalea was out of range. With his breath caught and held in his throat, Hawk weighed the knife in his hand. He'd practiced throwing it at least a thousand times while in Afghanistan. He'd been the best of all the members of his team. All he had to do was hit the carotid artery, and it would be all over for Kalea's captor.

Kalea's captor couldn't hold onto her as her body slumped to the ground. He tried to pull her up by her arm, but she slid further down his body.

Hawk chose that moment to throw his knife. His aim was true as the heavy military knife tore through the other man's skin to lodge in his neck.

The stranger holding Kalea released her and clapped a hand to the knife sticking out of his throat. He pulled it hard, tearing it free. Blood poured from the wound, running down his neck and chest onto Kalea's inert form. Pressing a hand to his neck, the man pointed his gun at Kalea.

A shot went off.

Hawk flung himself at the shooter, hitting him in the midsection.

Another shot sounded next to Hawk's ear.

The force with which Hawk hit the man was such that he knocked him off his feet and hit the ground flat on his back, hard. The gun flew from his fingers and clattered to a stop a couple yards away, well out of reach.

Kalea's captor lay on the ground beside her, blood flowing unchecked from the wound in his neck. His face paled, and his eyes remained open, unseeing.

Hawk leaped to his feet and retrieved his knife, prying it from the attacker's hands.

Then he knelt beside Kalea, brushing a hand over her hair, looking for wounds and signs of breathing. "Kalea?" he spoke softly, searching her body for a gunshot wound. There was blood…lots of it. Thankfully, it wasn't hers. He shook her shoulder. "Kalea, talk to me."

When she didn't move, he pressed two fingers to the base of her throat and waited for that reassuring sign of life…a pulse.

When he could feel nothing against his fingertips, his CPR training kicked in, and he immediately started chest compressions. He couldn't remember if breathing was still something he needed to do to resuscitate a victim. But he'd try everything in order to keep the woman he was falling in love with alive.

"Please, Kalea, breathe," he whispered as he pinched her nose and blew a breath into her mouth.

A hand clamped down on his shoulder.

Hawk spun, fists clenched to find Hank Patterson standing beside him, holding a rifle in his other hand.

"I'll do chest compressions." Patterson dropped to his knees beside Kalea and laid the weapon on the ground. "You breathe."

Together, they settled into a rhythm, feverishly pumping life back into Kalea's unmoving body.

Six compressions in, Kalea moved on her own.

Patterson rocked back on his heals. "I think she's coming out of it."

"Come on, Kalea, sweetheart, breathe." Hawk pressed his lips to hers and forced air into her lungs one more time.

Before he could raise his head, her arms wrapped around his neck and pulled him closer. The life-breathing kiss turned into a real kiss.

"Yup, I think she's back." Patterson chuckled.

"Coast Guard will be here any minute," another voice sounded behind Hawk.

He glanced up to see another man he recognized from way back, in his early days as a Navy SEAL. "Swede?"

The tall, blond man grinned. "Hey, Hawk. Glad to see you're still alive. We were worried for a while there. Good thing Patterson still has some mad skills as a sniper."

Hawk looked up into Hank's eyes. "Two shots?"

Patterson nodded. "One was mine. The other was his." He sucked in a deep breath and let it out. "I almost hit you. Had you lunged a second earlier, you would have been lying there instead of him. But if you hadn't hit him when you did, that bullet he shot could have found Miss Parkman." His new boss glanced down at Kalea. "Did you check her over? Is any of this blood hers?"

"I checked." Hawk shook his head. "None of it's hers." He smiled down at Kalea. "Do you hurt anywhere?"

She rubbed her chest and neck. "Nothing that won't

mend," she said, her voice hoarse. "What happened?" Kalea struggled to sit up.

Hawk slipped an arm around her back and helped. "I went down to check on your plane and found a boat. I hightailed it back up here, but he already had you." He shook his head. "I think I lost ten years off my life when he choked you until you passed out." Tipping his head toward Patterson, he nodded. "Kalea, this is my boss, Hank Patterson of the Brotherhood Protectors. He's a Navy SEAL, as well."

She looked beyond Patterson to the other man standing over them.

"Swede is another Brotherhood Protector."

Kalea leaned into Hawk. "I don't care if you're all flying purple people eaters, thanks for saving my life." She turned to look at the man on the ground behind her. "Is he…?"

"Dead," Patterson said.

"Damn," she muttered. "I never got him to tell me who he was working for." She looked into Hawk's eyes. "He was going to kill us both."

Hawk nodded. "He's not going to kill anyone, now."

"Yeah, but someone hired him. Whoever that is will come after us again." Kalea clutched Hawk's hand. "You're growing on me, cowboy. I can't lose you." A tear slipped from her eye and slid down her cheek.

Hawk's heart clenched in his chest. "Babe, I'm not going anywhere. We'll figure this out."

"Uh, for that matter," Patterson cleared his throat. "That's why we're here."

Kalea and Hawk glanced up at Patterson as he rose to his feet.

He gave a chin lift toward Swede. "No sooner had we gotten off the phone with you last night, then we got hold of the security camera footage from the hardware store in Hilo. We had a clear image of this guy." He jerked his thumb toward the man lying dead on the ground. "We did a facial scan through several criminal databases and came up with a match. Jordan Buckley, aka "Butch". He's been in and out of jail several times for aggravated assault and cruelty to animals. He's also known in Wyoming for having trained with a white supremacist group. He's skilled in all kinds of weapons and hand-to-hand combat."

Hawk swallowed hard. Kalea was lucky to be alive. The man could just as easily have snapped her neck rather than choke her to death.

"And we found something else on those security videos," Patterson said. "He was talking to someone else, exchanging what we think was money."

"Who was he?" Kalea asked, her eyes rounded. "Who wanted me dead?"

"It wasn't a he," Swede said. "It was a woman with blonde hair. We looked through more footage and found her getting into a car. We were able to capture an image of half of the license plate."

"We ran it by the Hawaii Motor Vehicle Division and came up with a match."

"Clarise Sanders," Kalea said, her voice tight, her lips thinning. "The bitch." Her eyes widened. "Has anyone gone after her?"

"No one knows but us, at this point." Patterson reached a hand down and helped Kalea to her feet. "We wanted to get to you first, so we hopped on a plane yesterday and flew out to Honolulu. We were getting off the plane when we got a call from your father, telling us your plane never made it to Oahu."

Hawk stood beside Kalea, his arm around her, holding her steady.

"Thankfully, Hawk had a GPS tracker on him, and we were able to locate you on this island." Swede waved a hand-held GPS tracking device. "We knew exactly where you were."

"But the storm delayed us getting here until this morning." Patterson grinned. "We pulled some strings and worked with the local Navy SEAL training group to get us to Maui, and then from Maui to here. They're waiting at the cove until the Coast Guard takes over the rescue operation."

The thumping sound of rotors beating the air sounded in the distance, moving toward them.

Moments later, an orange helicopter flew overhead and hovered, the rotor wash stirring up dust and debris. Slowly, the chopper lowered until it landed fifty yards away from the building and the people standing outside.

A couple Coast Guardsmen rushed toward them, carrying a stretcher basket.

It only took a few minutes for them to load Kalea into the chopper. Hawk insisted on going with them. Patterson and Swede assured him they would catch a ride back to Honolulu with the Navy SEALs.

Hawk stayed with Kalea, knowing his services

wouldn't be needed as soon as they cornered Clarise. His time with Kalea was nearing an end, which made him want to slow time and hang onto her as long as he could.

THE COAST GUARD medic had wanted Kalea to lie on the stretcher for the ride back to Oahu, but she'd insisted she was up to sitting in a seat for the trip back. She sat beside Hawk and let them buckle her safety harness around her.

As they lifted off the ground, Kalea squeezed Hawk's hand. The USCG crew had given them headsets to wear on the ride to Honolulu. Kalea stared down at the water, tears slipping from her eyes. "I take it my plane wasn't in the cove?"

Hawk's hold tightened on hers. "Sorry, babe. Buckley cut the line and set it adrift."

Kalea nodded. "I'll need to notify my father. He'll have someone out there looking for her as soon as possible." She looked out at the blue sky. "At least the storm moved on. We have a chance of finding her before she's torn apart by waves. He was so proud of his gift to me."

Hawk shook his head, a smile tugging at his lips. "Your father won't care about that plane, as long as you're okay."

She smiled. "I know. But I love that he got it for me. Even though he worried about me flying, he did it anyway. He knew how much flying meant to me."

"Your dad sounds awesome," one of the Coasties said. "I wish my dad would buy *me* a plane."

"At least you knew your dad," another Coast Guardsman said.

"What are you talking about?" the first Coastie asked. "I've met your dad. He's awesome."

The banter between the servicemen continued until they landed in Honolulu.

Kalea was transferred to a waiting ambulance. Hawk slipped in with her, and they arrived at the hospital a few minutes later. After two hours in the ER, Kalea was cleared by the doctor with a prescription for pain killers and instructions for taking it easy.

By the time she was released from the hospital, Hank Patterson and Swede arrived.

Kalea had contacted her father, urging him to stay on the Big Island when he'd wanted to fly in as soon as he'd heard she was there. Instead, he arranged for a charter flight service to pick up all four of them at the Honolulu airport and fly them to Waimea. He'd be waiting for them there.

The flight to the Big Island was a lot less traumatic than the aborted flight to Oahu. Kalea held her breath as they flew past Kaho'olawe, her gaze searching the ocean for her missing plane. Alas, she didn't see it in the vast expanse of water.

"You're alive," Hawk reminded her. "That's what matters."

"I know." She sucked in a breath and blew it out. "And we still have to deal with Clarise."

"Did you warn your father?"

She shook her head. "I didn't want Clarise to know we knew. I told him not to tell anyone I was alive, including Maleko and Clarise. I want to devise a plan to get her to spill her guts."

"What did you have in mind?"

Kalea squared her shoulders. "I want to confront her by myself."

Hawk shook his head. "I don't trust her."

"I think she likes having other people do her dirty work." Kalea had been rolling her thoughts over and over in her mind. "I don't think she'll have the nerve to try to kill me herself."

"I'm not willing to take that chance."

Kalea smiled. "You don't have a say. Remember? You quit as my bodyguard."

"Wait...what?" Patterson leaned over the back of Hawk's seat. "What's this about you quitting the Brotherhood?"

"I quit so I could be with Kalea without compromising the integrity of my mission."

"That's the biggest bunch of hooey I've ever heard," Patterson said. "Besides, I don't accept your resignation. You still work for me, and I haven't released you from your assignment."

Hawk raised an eyebrow and aimed his gaze at Kalea. "You heard the boss. I didn't quit after all."

"And I have a knack for getting my way." She lifted her chin. "I'm going after Clarise. That lady is going down." She snorted. "Try to kill my bodyguard, will she? I'll show her who has a backbone, and then some."

Hawk groaned. "I have a feeling we're going into rough weather, again."

Kalea stared out the window of the plane. "The sky is perfectly blue and clear. I don't know what you're talking about."

"It goes along with the saying, *The only easy day was yesterday.*"

The pilot came over the loudspeaker, announcing that they were landing and to buckle their seatbelts.

Kalea pulled hers tight and set her jaw. She'd get Clarise for trying to kill her and Hawk and make her pay by going to jail. A smile lifted the corners of Kalea's lips. She wondered how Clarise would feel about wearing orange. Somehow, she expected the woman wouldn't be too happy.

CHAPTER 15

Hawk wasn't too happy about Kalea's plan to out Clarise, but there was no stopping the woman when she got something in her head. At least he had the support of his new teammates to help protect Kalea should Clarise try her hand at murder.

Parkman had been ecstatic to see his daughter and almost blew their cover from the get-go.

Kalea had commandeered Patterson's black leather jacket and a baseball cap the pilot carried in his flight bag. Jamming her hair up into the cap and hunching down into the oversized jacket, she looked like a man. A small man, but nothing like the pretty Hawaiian princess she was.

Hawk had to remind himself he couldn't put his arm around her as they exited the chartered aircraft and crossed the tarmac to the waiting large SUV.

As they approached, Parkman got out of the back seat, smiling broadly. "Where is she? Where's my daughter?"

"Mr. Parkman, can we talk to you inside the vehicle?" Patterson gripped the man's elbow and ushered him to the back door.

Parkman shook loose of Patterson's grip. "What's wrong? What happened to my daughter?" He started to push past them to the airplane, but Kalea stepped in front of him.

"Dad," she whispered. "It's me. Get in the car. Now."

Her father stared down at her, blinking in the glare of the sun. "Kalea?"

"Get in the car," she repeated, gripped his arm and manhandled him into the back seat. Once he was in, she sat beside him and closed the door.

Patterson and Swede got in the other side and clambered into the third row of seats.

Hawk got in beside Mr. Parkman and closed the door. "Head for the Parkman Ranch," he said to Maleko, who happened to be driving.

Maleko shifted into drive and pulled away from the Waimea airport.

Once they were outside of the little town and headed to her home, Kalea held her father's hands in hers. "Dad, I don't want anyone to know I'm alive and back at the ranch just yet."

"Okay…" He stared down at where their hands joined. "I'm just thankful you were spared in that storm. I have people searching for your plane. I hope they'll find it soon."

"Thank you, Daddy." She leaned over and kissed her father's cheek. "I'm sorry I worried you."

"If it makes you feel better," Hawk said, "she did a

superb job landing the plane in a cove off Kaho'olawe." He hadn't been nearly as calm as she'd been as she'd glided in to land on the water.

"I think I died a thousand deaths through the night," her father said, squeezing her hands so hard they were going numb.

Kalea stared into her father's eyes. "The good news is that we survived."

"And as far as I'm concerned, that's all the news I need," her father said, pulling her back into his arms for a tight hug. "Planes can be replaced. I can't replace you." He kissed the top of her head and set her away from him. "Continue. I want to know everything."

"My plane was sabotaged, Dad. Whoever did it knew I was going to Oahu and got in the plane to monkey with my fuel and radio." She filled him in on the rest of what had happened from the attacks in Hilo and Waimea to almost being choked to death by Jordan Buckley.

All the while she spoke, her father's face grew paler and paler. He clutched her hand, his own shaking. When she finished, he swallowed hard. "This can't continue. Do you know who might be behind Buckley's attack?"

Kalea looked past him to Hawk then over her shoulder to Patterson and Swede.

Hawk spoke up. "We think we do. But we'll need your help to get her to confess."

Parkman frowned. "Her?"

Hawk nodded. "Her. Hank and Swede reviewed

security camera footage from the hardware store in Hilo. Buckley took money from a blonde woman."

Swede leaned across the back of the seat. "I downloaded a clip on my cell phone." He hit the play button and showed them a woman with long, straight blond hair handing a slim packet to Buckley. She paused to flip her hair over her shoulder in the same manner Clarise did.

"That could be any blonde," her father argued.

"Dad, what other blonde is there who would do this?" Kalea asked. "A woman with the most to gain."

"What does Clarise have to gain by your death?" her father asked, his voice cracking on the last word.

Kalea shook her head with a gentle smile that made Hawk's heart skip several beats. "Dad, you're quite a catch. Can't you see she's been flirting with you, coming over often, making menu decisions without your consent. She's vying for the position of Mrs. Parkman. Only one thing is standing in her way…"

Her father shook his head. "You're not standing in the way of anyone."

"I love you, Dad, and I want you to be happy. If you find a woman to love, and who loves you, I'm all for you remarrying." She cupped her father's cheek. "Mama wouldn't have wanted you to be alone the rest of your life."

"Then why would she think you were in the way and go to such extremes as to try to…," he swallowed hard, "kill you?"

"She has 130,000 reasons," Kalea said, her jaw hard, her lips pressing into a thin line.

Her father's eyes widened. "You think she wants control of Parkman Ranch?"

Kalea stared at her father for a long moment before answering. "I'm your only child. When you die, I get the ranch...unless you remarry."

"But I have it going into a trust. I had our attorney set it up that if I died, you'd get everything in the trust."

"And if I'm not around to claim it, but you have a wife by then, your wife would get everything."

"I'm not married." His frown deepened. "I still think it's a stretch. I find it hard to believe Clarise would go to such lengths to get control of Parkman Ranch."

"We'd like to know for certain as well," Hawk said. "Right now, it's all conjecture and a blurry picture of a blonde handing something to Buckley."

As they pulled through the gate to the ranch, Hawk, Kalea, Hank and Swede laid out their plan on the long winding drive through the property.

When they drove up to the ranch house, Hawk's gut clenched, and he realized the plan would go into place sooner than they'd expected.

Clarise's SUV was parked in the driveway.

Mr. Parkman squeezed his daughter's hands. "I don't know if I can pull this off. If Clarise truly is behind everything that happened, I'll want to wrap my hands around her throat and squeeze as hard as I can. How could she? I love you more than life itself."

Kalea hugged him quickly and ducked low in the seat. "You can do this. We have to know for sure. If she's behind Buckley and Nate's actions, she can't get away with what she's done." She waved toward the house. "Go. And remember, you're heartbroken."

"Be careful," Hawk said. "I don't like leaving you for even a few minutes."

"Maleko will look out for me," Kalea reassured him.

Hawk went along with the plan, counting the seconds until he could be with Kalea and know she was safe.

THE MEN PILED out while Kalea hunkered low on the floor.

When they were out, Maleko drove the SUV around to the garage and pulled inside. He got out, checked all around for anyone hiding inside before he opened the back door and helped Kalea out of the vehicle.

"Thank you, Maleko." She hugged him and hurried to the back door of the garage.

"Where are you going?" he asked. "I thought you were staying here until they got the confession out of Miss Sanders."

"I want to be there to hear it." She shot a glance over her shoulder to Maleko. "I won't let her see me."

Maleko frowned. "It was not part of the plan."

"I promise, I won't do anything stupid."

"You're changing the plan. No one knows." Maleko shook his head.

Kalea couldn't wait. She had to hear for herself what Clarise would say to her father. "I'll be okay." When she left the garage, the sun had set beyond the horizon, and the gray dusk provided just enough light to get her around until the stars came out in full force.

Kalea sneaked up to the house and waited in the bushes below the deck outside her father's study. The light inside the house made it easy for her to see who was there. The open window allowed her to listen to the conversation going on between her father and Clarise. The other men would have gone up the stairs to their rooms, giving Kalea's father a chance to talk alone with Clarise. If she didn't come out and tell him what they suspected was true, Hawk, Patterson and Swede would join them and show her the proof they had in the copy of the security camera video.

Clarise was talking. "John, I'm so very sorry about Kalea. I know how much she meant to you."

Her father shook his head. "I can't believe she's gone." He pounded his fist into his palm. "I won't believe it."

"You know how she loved flying. At least she went doing what she loved."

"We don't know for sure she's gone. They haven't found the plane."

"Darling," Clarise touched his arm, "that's a big ocean out there. The chances of finding her are...well, not good."

"She could have landed on one of the other islands."

"I don't see how," Clarise said. "If she had any trouble with the engine, she would have had very few options of where to put down."

"She would have sent out a radio call if she had trouble. She knows the drill. She would have sent out a mayday call." Kalea's father turned away from Clarise and stared out the window.

Kalea felt as if he was staring right at her.

Clarise went to him, slipping her arm around him. "She couldn't send out a mayday call if her radio quit working."

Her father turned toward Clarise, his eyes narrowing. "How would you know if her radio wasn't working?"

Clarise frowned. "It only makes sense. If she had engine trouble, she would have sent a radio call out to the ATC. If the ATC didn't receive such a call, obviously, her radio wasn't working." She shook her head, a slight smile curling the corners of her lips. "She would have called."

"If her radio was working…" Her father nodded. "Unless someone sabotaged her radio."

Clarise's brow dipped. "Who would have sabotaged her radio?"

Her father stared down at Clarise. "The same person who would have sabotaged her engine."

Clarise stepped backward, shaking her head. "Again, who would have done that? Everyone loved Kalea."

"Is that right?" John Parkman faced Clarise. "Did you love my daughter?"

Clarise raised a hand to her throat. "Why do you ask? You know I care about anything you care about. John," she touched his arm again, "I don't just work for you…I care about you. Losing your daughter has to be the worst thing that could happen to a father. I'm here for you. If you need to be angry, go ahead, take it out on me. I'm not going anywhere."

"I'm angry, all right. Someone has been trying to kill my daughter. That someone hired Nathaniel Bowman to give it a shot. He failed, so the person who hired him killed him to keep him quiet and hired someone else to do the job." He took Clarise's hand in his and held it tight. "Do you know anyone who might have hired Nate or the new guy, Jordan Buckley?"

Clarise pulled her hand free and stepped back. "John, I don't know what you're talking about."

"Clarise, only a very few people knew my daughter was flying out yesterday morning."

"Are you accusing me of tampering with her plane?" Clarise shook her head. "I don't know anything about planes, for one. And why would I hurt someone who means so much to you? I love you, John. I would never hurt you or anyone you care about."

Her father's jaw tightened. "Clarise, did you know there are security cameras throughout the parking lot of the hardware store in Hilo where Kalea was attacked the first time?"

Clarise shook her head, her cheeks draining of color. "No. Why do you ask? Why should I care?" Her voice shook. "John, you're scaring me."

"Clarise, you should be scared." He gave a slight nod toward the door to his study.

Hawk entered, carrying what appeared to be an electronic tablet in his hand.

"Do you want to see what was on the video in the parking lot of that hardware store?"

Clarise shook her head. "John, I didn't attack your daughter."

"I know that," Kalea's father said. "But the man who did met with someone prior to attacking Kalea. Would you like to see the video of that person handing a packet to the man who tried to kill my daughter? The same man who tried to kill her this morning?" He waved toward Hawk. "You remember Jace Hawkins, don't you?"

Clarise spun toward the door, her eyes widening. "What the—? How—?"

"How am I alive when I was in the plane Kalea was flying?" Hawk shook his head. "Because Miss Parkman is an excellent pilot. Even when the engine was sabotaged, she was able to land the plane successfully. And your mercenary wasn't successful in finishing us off. I'm sure he would be more than willing to tell the police what he knows."

Clarise shook her head. "You can't prove anything," she said, her voice strained and high pitched, unlike her usual calm tones.

"I think we can," Hawk said. "We have video footage of someone paying Jordan Buckley prior to his attack on Kalea in Hilo. And we have the license plate of the SUV that person drove off in."

"You know what vehicle we're talking about," Kalea's father said, his tone dark and deep. "You know, because it was you."

Clarise grabbed her purse and slung it over her shoulder. "I don't have to listen to this. I've never been so insulted in my life. We've worked together for more than five years. You'd think you knew someone." She fiddled in her purse, jingling her keys.

"I thought I knew you," Kalea's father said.

Kalea's heart hurt for her father. He trusted his employees. To find one who'd not only lied to him, but had attempted to kill his only daughter, had to be tearing him apart. Kalea wanted to punch the woman in the face for destroying her father's faith in his people.

Clarise straightened, pulling her hand out of her purse, along with a small gun in her palm. She aimed it at Hawk. "Get out of my way."

Kalea's heart skipped several beats and slammed into her ribs with a force that actually stung. That woman was pointing a gun at the man who'd found his way into Kalea's heart. She couldn't let the bitch kill him. She wouldn't. Kalea leaped out of the bushes and up onto the deck.

"Clarise, put the gun away," Kalea's father said. "It's over. The police are on their way. The video has been sent to the detective who's been in charge of the investigation from the start. Your license plate was matched to the one in the video."

"You can't stop me. I won't go to jail." She raised the barrel of the pistol, pointing it at Hawk's chest. "If you were with Kalea and you survived the plane crash, where is the little princess?"

"Here," Kalea said, and burst through the French door into her father's study. "I'm here."

Clarise spun toward Kalea, her gun turning with her.

Hawk sprang forward with the electronic tablet and slammed it down on Clarise's hand with the gun. The gun went off, but the bullet hit the floor. Hawk jerked it out of her hand, dropped the magazine out of the handle and cleared the chamber. "Ms. Sanders, I believe your ride has arrived."

Flashing blue lights shone through the study as Hawaii's finest arrived on the scene.

Clarise dodged around Hawk and ran for the door, only to be stopped by Patterson and Swede, standing in her way. "No. This can't be happening," she screeched. She turned to face Kalea's father. "They were supposed to die. You were supposed to marry me." Tears streamed down her face. "You ruined it," she screamed and ran toward Kalea, her fingers curled like claws, aiming for Kalea's face.

Hawk grabbed her from behind and clamped her arms to her sides. "You're done here."

The police entered the room and took Clarise in custody.

An hour later, after they'd given their statements and Clarise had been taken away, Kalea hugged her father goodnight and stepped out onto the porch.

The stars shone brightly, and the sky was so clear she swore she could see fever.

"The stars shine like this in Montana," Hawk's voice said from the corner of the porch.

Kalea turned toward him.

He leaned against the rail, his ankles crossed in front of him and his arms crossed over his chest.

"Shouldn't you be packing?" Kalea asked.

"I'm in no hurry," he said.

"I thought you wanted to get back to Montana,"

Kalea said and looked out again at the stars, afraid if she continued to stare at Hawk, the tears she'd been holding at bay would slip free of her eyes and slide down her cheeks. And she couldn't do that. She couldn't cry in front of a man she'd only met a few short days before. He'd been her bodyguard. Now that the threat was gone, his services were no longer required.

A sob rose up Kalea's throat. She swallowed hard to keep it from escaping, only managing to form a knot that hurt her vocal cords.

"Are you in a hurry to get rid of me?" Hawk asked.

She shook her head, unable to force words out. The tears she'd tried to hold back spilled over the edges and slid down her face.

"Kalea...look at me," he commanded.

She shook her head, that sob finally making its way out on a shaky hiccup.

Then arms surrounded her and pulled her back against him. "Hey. Why the tears?"

"Because," she whispered.

He turned her to face him and tipped up her chin. "Are you crying because my job here is done?"

She shrugged. "Maybe."

"About that..."

Kalea stared up into his eyes, her vision swimming in her tears.

"I really did turn in my resignation with Patterson."

Her tears froze, and her breath caught in her throat. "You did?"

He nodded. "I did." Then he shook his head. "He refused to accept it...again."

Her brow dipped. "How can he do that?"

"I told him he couldn't." Hawk cupped her cheeks in his palms and brushed his thumb across her lips. "But he offered me an alternative."

Kalea could barely concentrate when he touched her like he was. "Alternative?"

"Uh huh," he whispered, lowering his head until his lips were barely skimming hers. "He asked me if I wanted to start a branch of Brotherhood Protectors here in Hawaii."

Her heart beat faster, and she curled her fingers into his shirt. "And you said?"

"I'd think about it."

Kalea stiffened in his arms. "Don't you know what you want to do?"

"I do, but I wasn't sure about you."

"Me?" She shook her head. "What does starting a branch of Brotherhood Protectors in Hawaii have to do with me?" She could think of only one thing, but she had to hear it from him. She waited, her breath lodged in her lungs, her entire world on hold, waiting for his answer.

"I wasn't sure you wanted me to stick around. You see, you don't need me anymore."

"What are you talking about?" She gripped his shirt in her hands and pulled him closer, until their noses almost touched. "Call it love at first sight or lust, whatever it is, I need you like I need to breathe. If you want me to say it, I will. I think I'm falling for you. And I've never felt so happy in my life." She leaned up on her toes and kissed his lips. "Please tell me you'll stay.

Please. Because if you don't, I might have to consider moving."

He laughed. "Moving? Where to?"

"Montana, if that's where you want to go. Although, why you'd want to live in Montana when we have everything your heart desires right here in Hawaii, I don't know." She gazed up into his eyes. "So, what's it to be, *paniolo*? Are you going to stay here and see where this thing we have between us goes? Or am I going to have to pack my bags and follow you to Montana?"

He cupped the back of her neck and smiled down at her. "You'd do that for me?"

"No, I'd do it for me. I'm selfish that way. When I want something, I go after it with my whole heart." She drew an X over her chest. "And you just might have stolen my whole heart. I might need it back. Or at least share it with you." She laughed. "I'm babbling. I'll shut up now."

"It's like you said, what does Montana have that I can't find here in Hawaii? I can tell you one thing for sure." He brushed his lips across hers in a feather-soft kiss. "It doesn't have you."

"You're staying?" she asked, her happiness bubbling up her chest.

One side of his mouth quirked upward, and his gaze bore down into hers. "I had a talk with your father. He said I could set up an office in one of the buildings on the ranch. I guess that means I'm staying. Only one more question…"

"Yes!" she shouted, and then tamped down her excitement to ask, "I mean, what question?"

"Will you go out on a date with me? I'll let you choose where and how. And just so you know, I'm game for airplanes and horses."

"Since my plane is still missing, how about we go in a car and to a restaurant?"

"Deal." He kissed her again. "And one other thing," he said.

"Mmm," she mumbled, nibbling at his bottom lip.

"Will you dance for me? You know the dance you're practicing for the King Kamehameha celebration?"

"For you?" She laughed and hugged him close. "We'll have to find a place with a little more privacy."

"I know an island…" And he kissed her, holding her close like there might not be a tomorrow, and if there was, they would be together, sharing it.

SOLDIER'S DUTY

IRON HORSE LEGACY BOOK #1

Elle James
New York Times Bestselling Author

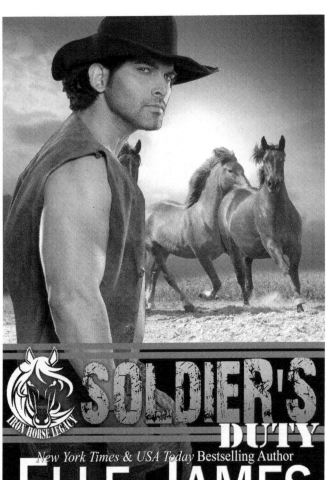

SOLDIER'S
DUTY

New York Times & USA Today Bestselling Author

ELLE JAMES

CHAPTER 1

"As you all know, William Reed escaped from a prison transport yesterday." Sheriff Barron stood in front of a group of men and women who'd gathered around him at the side of the highway in the foothills of the Crazy Mountains on a blustery cold day in early April.

He continued, "We have security camera footage showing him stealing a car from a convenience store in Bozeman. The license plate of the vehicle he stole matches the license plate of the vehicle behind me." Sheriff Barron turned to the side and waved toward a vehicle half-hidden in the brush behind him. "The state police are on their way, and they're also sending a helicopter from Bozeman. But they aren't as familiar with the mountainous terrain as you are, and the weather might keep them from using the chopper. That's why I've asked you to bring your horses and ATVs. All of you know these mountains better than anyone. And you are the select group of people I trust most to handle this situation."

James McKinnon tugged up the collar of his coat around his chin to keep a blast of wintery wind from snaking down his neck. He listened silently as the sheriff explained why they were there. With each breath James took, he blew out a little cloud of steam.

Rucker, his bay gelding, pawed at the ground impatiently.

James had chosen Rucker because he was the most sure-footed of the horses in his stable. For the manhunt they were about to conduct, the gelding was the best bet. The Crazy Mountains could be as dangerous as the man they were searching for. And the weather wasn't helping.

The sheriff gave them a steely glance. "We don't know at this point whether or not Reed is armed but assume that he is."

James's hand went to the pistol in the holster he had strapped to his hip.

"Sheriff, what do you want us to do?" one of the men in the crowd called out.

The sheriff straightened, with his shoulders pushed back and his mouth set in a firm line. He stared at each of the people gathered around, making eye contact with each person. "Bring him in."

"And how do you want us to do that," another man called out.

The sheriff's chin lifted. "Most of you follow the news. Reed was in prison for multiple counts of murder. He killed two guards during the armored truck robbery. When he was cornered, he killed two cops. The man was serving a life sentence without parole.

"While being transported to a high-security prison, his transport vehicle ran off the road. The driver was killed on impact, but the guard in back with Reed wasn't. He was injured. Reed finished him off. Now, I'm not telling you to kill Reed, but if at any time believe your life is in danger, shoot to kill the bastard. If at all possible, don't engage…report. Our primary goal is to bring Reed in before he hurts anyone else."

James's hands tightened into fists. He hadn't killed a man since he'd been a member of Delta Force more than two decades ago. Not that he'd become squeamish about killing a man in his old age, but it was just that he'd thought his people-killing days were over when he'd left the military.

The only killing he'd done lately was the occasional coyote in the chicken coop and deer or elk while hunting in the fall.

From the news reports he'd been following, he knew Reed had turned into a really bad character. James was glad the bastard had headed into the mountains instead of the city. He reckoned that if the convict was cornered, he would take whatever hostage he could to get out of a situation.

James had left instructions with his wife and daughter to stay inside the ranch house and keep the doors locked. But he knew they were stubborn women and wouldn't stand by and leave the animals to fend for themselves, especially in bad weather. They'd venture out into the barnyard to feed the chickens, pigs, horses and goats to keep them from going hungry. With the winter weather making a reappearance, they'd likely put some of the livestock in the barn.

Which would leave them at risk of being captured if Reed circled back to the Iron Horse Ranch. Hopefully, they'd be smart and enlist the help of their ranch foreman, Parker Bailey.

Sheriff Barron held up a paper with an image of William Reed. James didn't need to see the picture. He knew Reed. However, others amongst them were newer to Eagle Rock and the county. "This is our man. Right now, we think he's up in the mountains. The longer he's free, the hungrier he'll get. It's imperative we bring him in quickly. All of our families' lives are in danger as long as he runs free."

"Then let's stop talking and start tracking," Marty Langley called out.

The sheriff nodded. "All right, then, gather around the map. We're going to split up into different quadrants so we're not shooting at each other." Sheriff Barron spread a map over the hood of his SUV, and the group gathered around him. He gave instructions as to where each person would be during the hunt and what signal they should give if they found something. He handed out as many two-way radios as he had, distributing them to every other quadrant.

Once James had his assigned area, he mounted Rucker and rode into the mountains, his knee nudging the rifle in his scabbard, his hand patting the pistol on his hip.

He'd known Reed for years. When you lived in a small community, everyone knew everyone else. Some were better at keeping secrets than others but, for the most part, everyone knew everyone else's business.

Reed had been a regular guy, working in construction and hitting the bar at night. He'd been a ladies' man' with a lot going for him. How had a guy like that ended up robbing an armored truck and killing the people driving it? What had driven Reed down the wrong path?

James could have been home with his wife of thirty-five wonderful years, holding her close in front of the fireplace, instead of riding out on a cold winter's night in search of a killer.

He knew he had it good. After twenty years in the military, he'd settled in Montana on the land his father had passed down to him. He'd wanted his kids to have what he'd had growing up. Ranching had made him the man he was—unafraid of hard work, determined to make a difference, able to take on any challenge, no matter how physically or mentally difficult.

He'd been damned proud of his sons and daughter and how they'd taken to ranching like they'd been born to it. Even Angus, who'd been twelve when they'd moved to the Crazy Mountains of Montana. He'd been the first to learn to ride and show the other boys how wonderful it could be to have the wind in their faces, galloping across the pastures.

A cold wind whipped into James's face, bringing him back to the present and the bitterness of an early spring cold snap. Just when they'd thought spring had come and the snow had started to melt at the lower elevations, the jet stream had taken a violent shift downward, dipping south from Canada into the Rocky Mountains of Montana, dumping a foot of fresh snow all the way down into the valleys.

He nudged Rucker in the flanks, sending him up the path leading to a small canyon that crossed over a couple of ranches—including his, the Iron Horse Ranch.

He knew the area better than anyone, having lived on the ranch as a child and as an adult since he'd returned from serving in the Army. As his father's only child, he'd inherited the ranch upon his father's death. Now, it was up to him to make it sustainable and safe for his family and ranch hands.

Again, he thought about his wife, Hannah, and his daughter, Molly, and worried for their safety.

Clouds sank low over the mountaintops, bringing with it more snow, falling in giant flakes. The wind drove them sideways, making it difficult to see the trail ahead.

About the time James decided to turn back, he'd entered the canyon. Sheer walls of rock blocked some of the wind and snow, making it a little easier to see the path in front of Rucker.

James decided to give the hunt a little more time before he gave up and returned to the highway where he'd parked his horse trailer.

He knew of several caves in the canyon suitable for a fugitive to hole up in during a brutal winter storm. They weren't much further along the trail, but they were higher up the slope. Snowcapped ridges rose up beside him. He was careful not to make any loud noises that might trigger an avalanche. Spending the next couple days in a cave wasn't something he wanted to do.

If he survived an avalanche, he could make do with the natural shelter until a rescue chopper could get into the canyon and fish him out. But Hannah and Molly would be sick with worry. James tried not to put himself in situations that made his sweet wife worry. Unfortunately, the Reed escape had worry written all over it. The man had escaped. He'd already proven he'd kill rather than go back to jail. He wouldn't go peacefully.

Rucker climbed higher up the side of the canyon wall, following a narrow path dusted in snow. The wind blew the majority of the flakes away, keeping the rocky ground fairly recognizable.

The trail had been there for as long as James could remember. His father had told him it was a trail created by the Native Americans who'd once used the caves for shelter over a century ago.

Rucker stumbled on a rock and lurched to the side.

James's heart skipped several beats as he held onto the saddle horn.

Once Rucker regained his balance, he continued up the slope, plodding along, the snow pelting his eyes. He shook his head and whinnied softly.

James patted the horse's neck. "It's okay. Only a little farther, and we'll head back to the barn." The weather in early April was unpredictable. It could stop snowing altogether or become a white-out blizzard in a matter of minutes.

The first in the row of caves James remembered

appeared ahead and up the slope to his left. He dropped down from his horse's back and studied the dark opening. If he recalled correctly, the cave was little more than five or six feet back into the mountain side. Not enough to protect a man from the cold wind and driving snow.

James grabbed Rucker's reins and moved on to the next cave, glancing up the side of the hill as he approached.

The hackles on the back of his neck rose to attention. Had he seen movement in the shadowy entrance?

He stopped beside a small tree growing out of the side of the hill and looped Rucker's reins loosely over a branch. The horse wouldn't attempt to pull free. Rucker knew to hold fast. A loud noise might scare him into bolting for the barn. Otherwise, he'd stay put until James returned.

Pulling his handgun from the holster, James started up the incline toward the cave, his focus on the entrance and the overhang of snow on the slope above the cave. With the recent melting and the added layer of fresh snow, the snow above the cave could easily become unstable. Anything, including a gust of wind, could trigger an avalanche, sending snow and rocks crashing down the hillside.

James hoped he'd left Rucker well out of the path of the potential avalanche. If the snow started down the side of the hill, James would be forced to run for the cave and take shelter there. Possibly with a killer.

More reason to get up to the cave, check it out and get back down to Rucker as soon as possible. He should have turned back when the snow got so thick he could barely see the trail. If one of his sons or daughter had continued on, he would have reamed them for their irresponsible behavior. And here he was doing what he would expect them to avoid.

However, since he was there, he would check the cave. Then he'd head straight back to the highway and home. The search for the fugitive could continue the next day, after the snowstorm ended. Reed wouldn't make much headway in the current weather, anyway.

With his plan in mind, James trudged up the hill to the cave. He had camped in this particular grotto one fall when he'd been caught in a storm while out hunting elk. It went back far enough into the mountain to protect him from the wind and rain and was open enough to allow him to build a fire. He'd even staged additional firewood in case he ever got caught in a storm again. Then at least, he'd have dry wood to build a warming fire.

If Reed was up in this canyon, this cave would be the perfect shelter from the current storm. The next one in line was harder to find and had a narrower entrance.

As he neared the mouth of the cavern, he drew on his Delta Force training, treading lightly and keeping as much of his body out of direct line of fire as possible as he edged around the corner and peered into the shadows.

The sound of voices echoed softly from the darkness near the back of the cave. He smelled wood smoke before he spotted the yellow glow of a fire, shedding light on two figures standing nearby.

"Where is it?" one voice was saying, the tone urgent, strained.

"I'm not telling you. If I tell you, you have no reason to keep me alive."

James stiffened. He remembered having a conversation with Reed outside the hardware store in Eagle Rock several years ago. That husky, deep voice wasn't something a person forgot.

His pulse quickening, James knew he had to get back down the mountain to the sheriff and let him know what he'd found. They weren't supposed to engage, just report.

But he hadn't expected to find Reed with someone else. If he left and reported to the sheriff without identifying the other man and the two men managed to get out of the canyon before they were captured by the authorities, no one would know who was helping Reed.

"I got you out of there, the least you can do is share your secret."

"I put it somewhere no one will find it. If I die, it goes to the grave with me," Reed said. "I did that on purpose. I can't trust anyone. If you want to know where it is, you'll have to get me out of Montana alive."

"I told you I would. You have my word. But you can't leave Montana without it."

"No, but I can leave Montana without you. If I've learned one thing in prison," Reed's voice grew deeper, "the only person you can trust is yourself."

"Damn it, Reed, we don't have time to dick around. Sheriff Barron has a posse combing the mountains. The only thing keeping them from finding you is the storm moving in. Get the money, and let's get the hell out of here."

James strained to see into the darkness, but the man with Reed had his back to the cave entrance and appeared to be wearing a knit ski hat. The voice was familiar, but he couldn't put his finger on who it was. He leaned into the cave a little more, waiting for the man to shift into a position where the fire would light up his face.

"You know, there's a bounty on your head," the man told Reed, in a threatening tone. "Maybe I don't want your bag of money. It's probably marked anyway. I could turn you in and collect the reward. I'd have the money and be a hero for saving the world from a killer."

Reed lunged toward the other man, knocking him back, his face even deeper in the shadows, or was it covered in a ski mask? "You dare threaten me?" He lifted the man off his feet and shoved him against the wall. "Do you know the hell I've lived in for the past thirteen years? I've seen men like you who've had their tongues carved out with a spoon. I didn't get out of prison to put up with the likes of you."

The man being held against the wall gagged, his feet scraping against the hard rock surface behind him.

James couldn't let Reed kill the other man, even if the other man happened to be the one who'd helped him escape from prison. Taking a deep breath, he called out, "Drop him, Reed, or I'll shoot."

The convict froze with his hand still gripping the other man's throat. "Guess you're gonna have to shoot."

Then he spun, dragging his captive with him, and using his body as a shield.

Since his back was still to James, James couldn't see who it was.

"Go ahead," Reed taunted. "Shoot. This piece of shit deserves to die."

The man he held fumbled in his jacket pocket, pulled out something long and shiny and then shoved it toward Reed.

Reed gasped, his eyes widening. "Bastard," he said, his voice more of a wheeze. His grip loosened on his captive.

The man slumped to his knees and bent over.

Reed stood for a long moment, his hand curling around the knife protruding from his chest. He gripped the handle and pulled it out. He stared at it, and then at James, and collapsed on top of the man he'd almost killed.

James rushed forward, jammed his handgun into his holster and felt for a pulse in Reed's neck. He had one, but it was faint and fluttering erratically.

The man beneath him, grunted and pushed at the bulk of the dead man weighing him down. "Help me," he said.

James grabbed Reed's arm and pulled him off the other man, laying him flat on his back.

Reed stared up at James, his eyes narrowing. He whispered something.

James leaned close, barely able to hear.

"Where the...snake...threads...needle's eye," Reed

coughed, and blood dribbled out of the side of his mouth.

James pressed his hand to the wound in Reed's chest. Having seen similar wounds in Iraq, he figured the knife had damaged a major organ, and Reed wasn't going to make it out of that cave alive.

Reed raised a hand and clutched his collar in a surprisingly strong grip. "They'll never find it." He chuckled, a gurgling sound that caused more blood to ooze from the corner of his mouth. Then his hand dropped to his side, and his body went limp.

James pressed two fingers to the base of Reed's throat, feeling for a pulse. When he felt none, he started to straighten.

Something cold and hard pressed to his temple. "Move, and I'll shoot."

His heart hammering against his ribs, James reached for the gun at his side. A cold feeling washed over him that had nothing to do with the gale-force winds blasting down through the canyon outside the walls of the cave.

His holster was empty. He couldn't believe he'd helped the other man, only to have him take his gun and turn it on him.

"What did Reed say before he died?" the man behind him demanded.

James held up his hands, shaking his head. "I don't remember."

"You better start, or you can join him in his cold place in hell."

"Seriously, I couldn't hear what he said. It was all garbled."

"He said something about a needle. I know you heard him. Tell me." The angry guy behind him fired the gun, hitting James in the right arm.

Pain knifed through his arm, and it hung limp against his side.

"Tell me, or I'll shoot again."

Outside, a rumbling sound made James forget about being shot at again. "If you want to get out of this cave alive, we have to leave now."

"I'm the one with the gun. I say when we leave."

"Then you'll have to shoot me, because I'm not going to be trapped in this cave by an avalanche." James lurched to his feet and started for the entrance.

Rocks and snow started to fall from the slope above the cave's entrance.

"Avalanche," James called out.

The entire hillside to the south of the cave seemed to be slipping downward toward the floor of the canyon.

"Stop, or I'll shoot again!" the man in the ski mask yelled.

"That's what got the avalanche started in the first place. If you shoot again, even more will come crashing down on us." James kept moving toward the cave entrance, looking north at a narrow trail leading out of the other side of the cave from where he'd entered. "If you want to live, you better follow me, and for the love of God, don't shoot again." He'd figure another way out of this mess, if he didn't bleed out first. For now, James knew he had to get the hell out of there. If they stayed inside the cave, they'd be trapped. If they hurried out the north end, they might make it away from the avalanche.

Rocks and snow pelted his back as he hurried across the slippery slope, praying the bulk of the avalanche was well on its way to the south. But more snow and rocks rushed toward him and the man holding a gun on him. His head light from blood loss, James ran, stumbling and skidding across loose gravel and tripping over small boulders. A rush of snow and debris scooped his feet out from under him and sent him sliding down the slope. He fought to keep his head above the snow. Then he crashed into something hard and everything went black.

ABOUT THE AUTHOR

ELLE JAMES also writing as MYLA JACKSON is a *New York Times* and *USA Today* Bestselling author of books including cowboys, intrigues and paranormal adventures that keep her readers on the edges of their seats. When she's not at her computer, she's traveling, snow skiing, boating, or riding her ATV, dreaming up new stories. Learn more about Elle James at www.elle-james.com

Website | Facebook | Twitter | GoodReads | Newsletter | BookBub | Amazon

Or visit her alter ego Myla Jackson at mylajackson.com
Website | Facebook | Twitter | Newsletter

Follow Me!
www.ellejames.com
ellejames@ellejames.com

ALSO BY ELLE JAMES

Iron Horse Legacy

Soldier's Duty (#1)

Ranger's Baby (#2) TBD

Marine's Promise (#3) TBD

SEAL's Vow (#4) TBD

Brotherhood Protectors Series

Montana SEAL (#1)

Bride Protector SEAL (#2)

Montana D-Force (#3)

Cowboy D-Force (#4)

Montana Ranger (#5)

Montana Dog Soldier (#6)

Montana SEAL Daddy (#7)

Montana Ranger's Wedding Vow (#8)

Montana SEAL Undercover Daddy (#9)

Cape Cod SEAL Rescue (#10)

Montana SEAL Friendly Fire (#11)

Montana SEAL's Mail-Order Bride (#12)

Montana Rescue (Sleeper SEAL)

Hot SEAL Salty Dog (SEALs in Paradise)

Hot SEAL, Hawaiian Nights (SEALs in Paradise)

Brotherhood Protectors Vol 1

Hellfire Series

Hellfire, Texas (#1)

Justice Burning (#2)

Smoldering Desire (#3)

Hellfire in High Heels (#4)

Playing With Fire (#5)

Up in Flames (#6)

Total Meltdown (#7)

Declan's Defenders

Marine Force Recon (#1)

Show of Force (#2)

Full Force (#3)

Driving Force (#4)

Mission: Six

One Intrepid SEAL

Two Dauntless Hearts

Three Courageous Words

Four Relentless Days

Five Ways to Surrender

Six Minutes to Midnight

Hearts & Heroes Series

Wyatt's War (#1)

Mack's Witness (#2)

Ronin's Return (#3)

Sam's Surrender (#4)

Take No Prisoners Series

SEAL's Honor (#1)

SEAL'S Desire (#2)

SEAL's Embrace (#3)

SEAL's Obsession (#4)

SEAL's Proposal (#5)

SEAL's Seduction (#6)

SEAL'S Defiance (#7)

SEAL's Deception (#8)

SEAL's Deliverance (#9)

SEAL's Ultimate Challenge (#10)

Texas Billionaire Club

Tarzan & Janine (#1)

Something To Talk About (#2)

Who's Your Daddy (#3)

Love & War (#4)

Ballistic Cowboy

Hot Combat (#1)

Hot Target (#2)

Hot Zone (#3)

Hot Velocity (#4)

Cajun Magic Mystery Series

Voodoo on the Bayou (#1)

Voodoo for Two (#2)

Deja Voodoo (#3)

Cajun Magic Mysteries Books 1-3

Billionaire Online Dating Service

The Billionaire Husband Test (#1)

The Billionaire Cinderella Test (#2)

The Billionaire Bride Test (#3)

The Billionaire Matchmaker Test (#4)

SEAL Of My Own

Navy SEAL Survival

Navy SEAL Captive

Navy SEAL To Die For

Navy SEAL Six Pack

Devil's Shroud Series

Deadly Reckoning (#1)

Deadly Engagement (#2)

Deadly Liaisons (#3)

Deadly Allure (#4)

Deadly Obsession (#5)

Deadly Fall (#6)

Covert Cowboys Inc Series

Triggered (#1)

Taking Aim (#2)

Bodyguard Under Fire (#3)

Cowboy Resurrected (#4)

Navy SEAL Justice (#5)

Navy SEAL Newlywed (#6)

High Country Hideout (#7)

Clandestine Christmas (#8)

Thunder Horse Series

Hostage to Thunder Horse (#1)

Thunder Horse Heritage (#2)

Thunder Horse Redemption (#3)

Christmas at Thunder Horse Ranch (#4)

Demon Series

Hot Demon Nights (#1)

Demon's Embrace (#2)

Tempting the Demon (#3)

Lords of the Underworld

Witch's Initiation (#1)

Witch's Seduction (#2)

The Witch's Desire (#3)

Possessing the Witch (#4)

Stealth Operations Specialists (SOS)

Nick of Time

Alaskan Fantasy

Blown Away

Stranded

Feel the Heat

The Heart of a Cowboy

Protecting His Heroine

Warrior's Conquest

Rogues

Enslaved by the Viking Short Story

Conquests

Smokin' Hot Firemen

Love on the Rocks

Protecting the Colton Bride

Protecting the Colton Bride & Colton's Cowboy Code

Heir to Murder

Secret Service Rescue

High Octane Heroes

Haunted

Engaged with the Boss

Cowboy Brigade

Time Raiders: The Whisper

Bundle of Trouble

Killer Body

Operation XOXO

An Unexpected Clue

Baby Bling

Under Suspicion, With Child

Texas-Size Secrets

Cowboy Sanctuary

Lakota Baby

Dakota Meltdown

Beneath the Texas Moon

Made in the USA
Columbia, SC
19 March 2020